Findin

by

JoMarie DeGioia

PUBLISHED BY:

Bailey Park Publishing

ISBN: 978-0-9899801-1-1

Finding Harmony

Book One of the
Cypress Corners series

by

JoMarie DeGioia

Enjoy your visit to Cypress Corners.

JMarie DeGi

Chapter 1

Cypress Corners, Florida

"Hey!"

Harmony Brooks jumped at the deep voice, dropping her notes. She looked up at the large man looming in front of her and her heart stopped. *Adam.* She blinked up at him, tilting her head to one side to block the late afternoon sun shining over his broad shoulders. She took in a breath. Not Adam, thank God. His features were stronger than Adam's, and he looked to be about thirty. He *was* good looking. If you liked the polished type. Well, she didn't. Not anymore.

"May I help you?" she asked.

He stepped closer. "What are you doing on this site?"

She took a few steps back. The low plastic tape marking the edge of the work site hit her calves and she forced herself to stop her retreat. This wasn't Adam. This was just a stranger dressed in rugged outdoor clothes from an expensive catalog. Then she noticed where his big booted feet were planted. "Watch out, you're—"

"Listen," he cut in. "It's my job to secure this site.

This project was contracted months ago."

She pointed to the mound at his feet. "But you're-"

"And by my guess, miss, you're trespassing."

As he started to recite some rehearsed corporate line, she watched first one fire ant then another crawl up the perfect crease of his right pant leg. A few more joined the march over his pristine hiking boots and she opened her mouth to warn him again. Suddenly he cursed, slapping at his leg as he fell on his backside. She bit her lip for a moment, then she lost the struggle. She couldn't help it. She laughed.

"Son-of-a… !" he yelled. "What the hell?"

She quickly sobered and stepped over the tape to reach him. "Easy." She brushed away the few ants still clinging to his pant leg, lifting the cuff to make sure the culprits under it were gone too. She stood. "I think you're all right now."

"Damn." He pinned her with his gray eyes. "What was that? My leg's on fire."

She picked up her backpack and returned to him. "Fire ants," she said. "They can really sting."

He cursed again. "Really? I hadn't noticed."

She took out a water bottle and a spare T-shirt, pouring the water onto the cotton. "This will help cool the bites."

She crouched down and held the damp cloth to the red welts rising among the crisp dark hairs on his skin. He had a nice build. Why he bothered ironing his camp shirt and chinos was beyond her. He certainly had strong legs beneath those pressed pants. "Is that any better?"

He closed his eyes and nodded. She ran her gaze over him as he visibly relaxed. His hair was a glossy black, thick and rich, and he smelled delicious, crisp and musky. Clean-shaven cheeks couldn't hide the shadow of a beard on his square jaw.

"Yeah, that's better," he said. He opened his eyes. "Thanks, babe."

She gasped as she stared into his eyes. They were as gorgeous as the rest of him, a lovely gray like the lake on a cloudy day, and framed by black lashes. Then his hand covered hers and a prickling of heat shot up her arm, hotter than any fire ant's bite. She jerked away, leaving the T-shirt in his hand.

"Well." She pressed her hand against her belly. "Um,

what were you yelling about before the ants bit you?"

His compelling eyes turned flinty. "You're trespassing, miss. On my work site."

Back to that, then. Good. She could use the focus.

She straightened. "As much as I *hate* to break this to you, you can't build on this spot."

He came to his feet and nearly stepped on the ant mound again. She braced her hands on his chest and pushed.

His eyes widened as he stumbled and almost fell on his backside again. "What the—? What are you doing?"

"The ant mound, buddy," she said. "Sheesh."

Her palms tingled with the memory of the hard muscles beneath that ridiculously-crisp shirt and she fisted her hands. Oh, she could smell him again. She swallowed. Hard.

"Thanks." He cleared his throat. "We can't build here? Since when? Chapman Financial finalized the contracts for this job months ago."

"Things have changed." She focused on the scrubby plant to her left. "There's a protected species on this site."

He looked around, his brows drawn together. "I saw

some grasshoppers big enough to be batter-dipped and fried. They're protected?"

She shook her head and pointed to the wild buckwheat. "No. But this is." She gathered her notes and shook the sand off of them. "*Eriogonum longifolium.* A wild scrub buckwheat."

"Eriggigg… what?" He stared at her for a beat. "A plant? A friggin' plant?"

She braced a hand on one hip. "Look. I feel bad about the fire ants, but this plant is endangered and construction can't commence until the Cypress Corners Institute says so."

"That's ridiculous." He thrust the damp T-shirt toward her. "You can't make us stop because of one weed."

She grabbed the shirt from him. "It's not a weed," she said. "This is a valuable find."

He snorted. "Is this about money?"

She ran her eyes over his perfectly pressed clothes. "I'm not the one who bought out the Banana Republic."

He pulled back. "Maybe you're the one with her eyes on the cash."

She stiffened. "I don't raise funds for the Institute. I

certainly have no financial stake in the development, if that's what you're implying."

He shook his head. "I'm not implying anything, miss. The Institute approved this site and the Cypress execs signed off on it. We got the damn contract. We have to get the thing finished before the year's end."

"The Recreation Café," she said. "A snack bar so hikers can take a break for gourmet coffee before continuing on the nature trails. Yeah, I know all about it."

"Look, there are people I need to answer to. Believe me, honey. Some friggin' weed won't stand in our way."

"That's it," she said. "I don't have to listen to this. I answer to the Institute and not to you."

He smiled and, though handsome, it wasn't a pleasant expression. "We'll see. I'll speak with the developer. He'll get with the Institute and before you know it you'll be out of here on your cute little butt."

She blinked at the back-handed compliment. Cute little butt?

She lifted her chin. "Do what you want to do. But I'll do what I *have* to do."

He grabbed up his sunglasses and stalked back

through the brush, rubbing his leg as he limped a bit. She gave a sharp nod. Good for him.

She watched him for a moment, her heartbeat at last returning to normal. He was sexy. His butt wasn't so bad, either. His mood, on the other hand…

She shoved her notes into her backpack and zipped it closed. Another smooth city fool.

Well, she wouldn't make that mistake again.

***

Rick's leg was on fire. Fire ants? Beautiful. He hadn't counted on them. He hadn't counted on the plant girl either. When she'd put her hand on his leg she'd sent a spark straight up to his groin. He could still feel her hands on his chest, delicate and strong as she pushed at him.

She'd caught his eye immediately, framed by the pink tape marking off the construction site. A goddess dressed like the girl on the Crocodile Hunter. Curly honey-colored hair pulled back in a long ponytail that nearly touched the sweetest butt he'd ever seen, shown to perfection in worn khaki shorts. She wasn't tall, but what was there was nicely built. Shapely tanned legs, small feet in trim hiking boots. Mmm…

11

And her front looked even better than her back. Full, rounded breasts that pressed against her soft cotton shirt and a face like an angel framed by wispy curls she brushed back from her flushed cheeks as she wrote in that damn notebook.

She was gorgeous, with her hazel eyes flashing at him as she defended that ridiculous weed. An endangered plant? It was ridiculous.

He'd thought this job would be quick. Now she was going to delay his return to civilization for some scrubby plant? The hell with that. The contract was written and the café would be built. He'd talk to the Institute right away. He'd find a way to satisfy the contract.

He had to.

He climbed back into his borrowed golf cart and glanced at his BlackBerry. No service. Big surprise. He started the cart and spun sand and dirt with the wheels as he turned back toward the Welcome Center in the village of Cypress Corners. Sweat trickled down the back of his neck. Why was it so friggin' hot in October?

Cypress was a contradiction he couldn't figure out. Expensive homes, state of the art fitness and recreation and upscale retail space were bracketed by areas conserved for nature and wildlife. Strange.

This wasn't where he expected to be this fall. He was here to oversee the building and staffing of a nine-hundred-square-foot snack bar to satisfy his company's investors. He preferred Colorado or even Maine to Central Florida, but the company had to finish the job they started last year when they put their clients' money into the main restaurant and banquet facility. They had until the end of the year to collect the last installment, then planning could start in earnest on the recreation center slated for the lakeside.

His boss was counting on him, and Rick wanted to prove himself. He needed to prove himself. He'd just focus on doing what he did best: get in, get the job done and get the hell out.

He crossed back into cell service and his BlackBerry chirped. Back in the land of the living. As he neared the center, the cell rang. He stopped the cart and looked at the screen. Damn. The boss.

He jabbed the answer button. "Yeah?"

"Chapman?" the voice barked. "That you?"

He nodded. "Hey, Dad. Yeah, it's me."

He listened to his father's latest rant as he absently rubbed his burning leg. Bill Chapman was the kind of man you didn't interrupt, which pleased Rick at the moment because he didn't really want to talk to him.

"The snack bar should be started already," Rick's father said. "Tell me you saw the site today."

He thought about the plant angel again. Yeah, he saw the site.

"I did," he said. "But there's a problem."

"A problem?" He could practically feel Bill's irritation from there. "What kind of problem?"

He took in a breath. "The Institute says we can't build on that site."

"Bull," his father said. "That site was approved by the damn Institute, Rick. Get on it."

"I can't," he said. "There's this species of endangered plant—"

"A plant?" his father cut in. "This is about a *plant*?"

The echo of his earlier words struck him and he squeezed his eyes shut. Was this how he'd sounded to the plant girl?

"I'm working on it," he told his father. "I'll get with

the developers."

His father blew out a curse. "Good. I dealt with those tree-huggers at the Institute and got the main club and restaurant built. This should be easy, even for you."

He let the barb slide and thought of the girl again. Hot, spirited and self-righteous. Easy? He doubted that.

"Yeah, sure," he said.

"Damn it, I made promises," Bill went on. "Promises our investors are counting on me to keep."

Promises? Rick doubted his father had kept one to him in his whole life.

"They'll get their return, Dad," he said.

"They better," his father said. He took in a breath. "Ah, well."

He knew his father shifted gears and braced himself for what would come next.

"Are you coming up to Boston for Thanksgiving?" his father asked.

God, no. "I hadn't planned on it," he said.

"Tiffany would love to have you."

He didn't doubt that. Tiffany was his father's fourth and latest trophy wife, and she was no prize. She was clawing and manipulative and the reason he was in Central Florida right now instead of waiting for a more desirable project to open up. At least she was the most obvious reason.

"I doubt I'll make it, Dad," he said. "Work will keep me pretty busy here."

"Yeah, yeah," his father said. "The tree-huggers. Let me know what the Institute says. We're on a deadline, Chapman. Time is money."

He nodded, certain the call was over. He and his father had little to say to each other for the past fifteen years. This phone call wouldn't be any different.

"I'll call you after I meet with them," he said.

Without another word his father broke the connection. He stared at the phone for a moment, then pocketed it. Bill Chapman wasn't one to waste time on emotion or affection. Hadn't Rick's mother learned that lesson the hard way years ago?

He still felt the loss of his mother deeply, along with Bill's defection three years before that. He'd get this damn thing built and finally prove his worth to the old man. God, he was twenty-nine years old and one call from his father could make him feel like a little kid.

"Pitiful," he grumbled. He got out of the cart. He'd hit the beach and leave the deep thinking to tomorrow.

***

Harmony headed to her camp on the far side of the property to clean herself up before going to the Cypress Corners Institute. She adjusted her backpack on one shoulder and walked down the path, her sturdy boots making soft footfalls on the sand beneath her feet. Thick cotton socks cushioned her steps and the sun warmed her through her camp shirt. She tilted her face up to the sun and took in a breath, smelling earth and pine and fresh air. It almost make her forget the confrontation with the guy from Chapman.

It was October, but true autumn was months away. She loved Central Florida, especially the subtle change of seasons. Tourists seldom noticed the slight variations of color in their surroundings, focusing instead on the nearest theme park or closest beach. She pitied them, mostly Northerners cramming as much "fun" as possible into their weeks' vacation. Thankfully, few of them came here for their holiday. Cypress Corners didn't hold that kind of attraction for them. She, however, loved it.

She'd landed her dream job here five months ago, and it seemed her work as a plant conservationist would finally make a difference. The size of the property, sprawled over ten thousand acres of some of the prettiest land in the region, meant she had little human contact except for checking in at the Institute. That suited her just fine. Plants were much easier to figure out than people. Their needs were clear cut, no duplicity or manipulation in their world.

It was quite unusual that more than half the land was set aside as a sanctuary for native plants and animals, but that pleased her to her toes. The rest of it was dedicated to expensive homes, retail stores, and recreational facilities, but she felt no lure toward those aspects of the community.

The golf club and restaurant were quite upscale, in sharp contrast to what she felt was more important. But the Institute didn't operate in a vacuum, and money made it possible for more noble ideals to be realized. Who was she to question the Institute's arrangement with the developers?

The site for a snack bar designed to cater to those using the proposed nature trails was the area under contention today. She saw no need for such a thing. Self-sufficient, she had no problem carrying her own pack with whatever essentials she needs, whether she was hiking on Institute business or for her own pleasure. A "recreation café?"

"Maybe." She shrugged. "Maybe not."

Eriogonum longifolium, var. gnaphali folium. The leggy wild buckwheat right smack in the middle of the site would stop construction, at least for now. No matter what the Chapman guy said.

She'd see to it.

Chapter 2

Harmony's camp was wired for electricity and her tent-cabin had a separate plumbed bathroom and shower. The spot was slated to become a lakeside recreation area within the coming year, but for now it was hers and hers alone. Just the clear water, sprawling live oaks and towering cypress trees to keep her company.

Her tent-cabin wasn't large, just one room with a screened-off private area to change. The short walk to the bathroom and shower was no hardship. She knew where to step. Not like that fool she met yesterday.

She thought of the pain-in-the-butt corporate guy from yesterday and felt that tremble in her belly again. What was wrong with her? He was overbearing and cold. But when his hand had touched hers she hadn't felt cold. Oh, those eyes. So deep. His manner, on the other hand…

He was forceful and smooth, just like Adam. Well, she wasn't a naïve coed anymore. At twenty-six years old she knew better. She removed her ponytail holder and dragged a brush through her hair. She wouldn't be overwhelmed again. She certainly wouldn't be fooled.

Adam had been older than she, and he'd used his citified skills to woo her when she was in college. She'd never forgive herself for the loss of more than her heart. Her parents still had to work hard to recoup the money Adam had all but stolen from them with his scheme. So did she. They didn't know that. They never would. She should have protected them.

Thank goodness her salary allowed her to at least start to repay them. Little by little, the bank account she'd opened in their name was growing. It would never be enough, but hopefully in a few years she'd tell them about the account and take away some of their burden. As long as the guy from Chapman Financial didn't do anything to compromise her job.

She put Adam and her encounter with the guy from Chapman out of her mind and, after changing into fresh clothes, reviewed her notes on the wild buckwheat. She'd told the director about the plant yesterday, when she stopped at the Institute. He'd been excited, for the buckwheat grew in very few places in Central Florida. The sandy soil of the property was the perfect habitat for the plant. That was something she could definitely identify with.

After her mistake with Adam she'd thrown herself into her studies and a Master's Degree in Environmental Science was the result. She hadn't wasted a moment of her time at the University of Central Florida, not as an undergrad and not as a graduate student. She wouldn't waste her opportunity here. This job meant more than protecting endangered plants.

She stepped outside her cabin and walked around to the electric scooter plugged into an outlet behind it. The small trunk behind the seat accommodated the bag holding her notes and stuff and the scooter's fat tires made it perfect for her infrequent trips to the Institute. She stashed her bag and hopped on, fastening her bike helmet over her curls.

It didn't take long to reach the Village Center where the Institute was located. Her scooter tires bounced gently over the brick walk as she turned toward the Institute. The Center was pretty, and designed to serve as the heart of everything in Cypress Corners. With its charming retail stores and plenty of benches lining the walk for residents and visitors to sit, it was a popular spot. Though it was just a few years old, it had the feel and appearance of an old-fashioned small-town.

Several people took advantage of the place this afternoon. Children indulged in their quickly-melting ice cream at the quaint soda shop at one corner, couples and friends talked over coffee at tables set in front of the coffee shop, folks walked their dogs and called "hello" to people they passed. She received several nods of greeting but she doubted anyone outside the Institute knew her name. That didn't bother her. She preferred her solitude.

The one exception was Antoinette Fairfax. Hettie, as everyone in town called her, waved enthusiastically from her customary perch set near one corner of the outdoor space. Under the shade of a sprawling Crepe Myrtle tree, a tall glass of sweet tea held in her other hand, Hettie was hard to ignore. She wore a large straw hat only a woman born and raised in the South would ever wear, her bangs a silvery fringe beneath. A flower-print smock, denim overalls, and a pair of bright green Crocs completed her outfit. She was outrageous and sweet, and Harmony found it harder and harder to maintain her distance from this particular resident of Cypress Corners. She was in her seventies but looked closer to fifty. She claimed this was due to healthy living, big hats and the liberal application of sunscreen.

Harmony slowed her scooter to a stop at the railing beside Hettie's table. "Hi, Hettie."

"Hello, Harmony. Join me?"

Hettie waved to the chair opposite. It was piled with gardening magazines and seed catalogs, as was much of the tabletop in front of her.

Harmony smiled. "Sorry, I'm on Institute business."

Hettie's mouth turned down, then she waved a hand. "You're always on the go. I hope Doc Robbins knows the treasure he has in you."

Hettie referred to the Institute director, and Harmony hoped to prove herself worthy of the faith he put in her from her very first day.

"I love my job, Hettie."

Hettie's blue eyes narrowed, and for a moment Harmony feared she tried to read her aura or something. Goodness knows Harmony's mom was always doing that. To her relief, Hettie simply clicked her tongue.

"Your job. Yes, you love your plants." She held up the magazine closest to her. "I share that passion. But what about the other kind?"

She flushed, the hunky Chapman guy coming swiftly to mind. "I don't know what—"

"Men," Hettie crowed.

Two young mothers at a nearby table turned at the word, their brows arched. Harmony managed a smile at the women and faced Hettie. "I don't have time for men."

Hettie let loose with a laugh. "Girl, you have to make time. Why, when Mr. Fairfax was alive... " Her eyes sparkled. "Mmm, he was fine, Mr. Fairfax was." She winked at Harmony. "He knew how to get me to focus on something other than plants."

Harmony chuckled. "Hettie."

Hettie nodded. "Go on. Get to your precious Institute. All of us here in Cypress know how important that work is."

Harmony started her scooter. "See you, Hettie."

Hettie saluted her with her glass and took a long sip as Harmony continued on to the Institute. Hettie wasn't too far off with her last comment. The Institute was responsible for the Village Center, its agreement with the Cypress developers making sure the area didn't put nature last.

Plenty of native trees shaded the area and mounds of Florida wildflowers and plants lent color. She recognized most of them as she passed, bluestem and cupseed and cat briar. They were pretty despite their unusual names.

She parked her scooter outside the Institute and removed her helmet. She took her bag out of the trunk, walked up to the wide glass doors and stepped into the air-conditioned lobby.

"Hello, Miss Brooks," the receptionist said.

She smiled at the red-haired girl behind the desk. "Hi, Becky. Is the director in?"

Becky nodded. "Yes. I'll buzz him."

Harmony looked around the lobby as the girl spoke softly into the intercom. The sunlit space reflected the Institute's worthy agenda. Decorated in the colors of true Florida—rich greens, soft tans, and clear blues—it was filled with handmade rattan furniture and breathtaking photos of native flora and fauna hung on the textured walls. If she had to be inside, this was one place she could tolerate.

"Dr. Robbins said to go right in," Becky said.

Harmony nodded. "Thank you."

She passed the desk and turned down the hall toward the director's office. The door was ajar, not unusual for her boss and mentor. He sat hunched over his desk, poring over papers scattered on his desk. His glasses sat on his balding head as he nodded agreement at something he read. She rapped softly on the smooth maple door and his head shot up.

"Harmony!" He smiled, dimples showing in his cheeks. "Come in, come in."

She stepped inside and closed the door. She gestured at the papers. "I hope I'm not disturbing you."

"What?" He shook his head. "No, no. I'm just working through the latest expansion plans. The lakeside recreation center will take a lot of planning." He waved a hand toward the chair opposite him and stacked the papers into an untidy pile. "So tell me."

She nodded and settled into the chair. "It's definitely a scrub wild buckwheat."

Dr. Robbins blinked then grinned. "Good! Do you have photos?"

"No, I—"

"I know, I know. No digital camera." He opened a

drawer in the desk and pulled out a small silver camera. "Here. Take as many photos as you need. You can upload them here when you're finished."

She took the camera. She knew she should have a laptop and camera in her tent, but she preferred using the Institute's facilities. It gave her an excuse to go into the village. That realization surprised her.

"I'll ride out to the site and snap some pictures later today," she said.

She put the camera into her bag and settled back in the chair. Toying with the frayed cuff of her shorts, she tried to decide how to tell Dr. Robbins about the guy from Chapman Financial.

"I hear Chapman's field man paid a visit today," the director said.

She lifted her head to face him. Well, that was easy. "Yes," she said. "He wasn't pleased with my discovery."

Dr. Robbins laughed lightly. "I don't imagine so. He has investors to consider. Quite an interesting fellow, don't you think?"

He popped into her mind again, tall and strong and gorgeous. Interesting? Oh, yes. "I suppose."

Dr. Robbins narrowed his blue eyes on her and she felt her cheeks heat. "He called." He smiled again. "And according to Becky, he wasn't happy."

The guy's threat came back to her. *Out on her cute little butt,* he'd said. Her stomach dipped. Oh, no. She couldn't lose this job.

"Did he… stop by here?" she asked.

"No. He said something about heading to the beach."

A flash of him in nothing but swim trunks filled her mind for a moment. She'd felt that strong, broad chest when she shoved him away from the ant mound. Oh, my.

"That gives me a reprieve, then," she said. She came to her feet. "I'll get the photos and stop back here later."

Dr. Robbins stood. "Why don't you have dinner in the village, Harmony? A few of us are heading over to The Clubhouse, and—"

"No, thank you," she said quickly. "I'll make sure I'm back here before. What time are you going?"

"That wasn't what I—"

She waved her hand. "I'll be back in a little while, Dr. Robbins."

He opened his mouth to protest further, then nodded.

"Tomorrow is soon enough, dear. I'm trusting you to keep the habitat secure, Harmony."

She blinked. "Me? I thought I'd just get the proof and let the Institute take it from here."

"You have the knowledge. Your degree proves it. You have the spirit." He nodded. "I saw that when you were still in grad school. You're the one to keep Chapman Financial at bay until we find a solution to this dilemma. We can't have the buckwheat compromised."

She was the one? "I... Thank you, Dr. Robbins. I'll do what I can. I'll see you tomorrow, then."

Dr. Robbins nodded and she left the office. She stepped out into the bright afternoon. The director trusted her to keep Chapman Financial in line? To keep *him* from destroying the buckwheat? She was floored.

That's when she saw him again, standing in front of a shiny black SUV. A Hummer. Her lip curled. That figured. He was talking to one of the women who worked in the Sales Office, a tall leggy brunette who managed to look fresh and crisp despite the humidity. Well, years of working in artificial air would take its toll on her skin eventually.

As Harmony watched, the woman patted his arm then tossed her shining black hair as she sashayed back into the office. Harmony tugged on her own curls, out of control from the heat and the helmet. She hopped on her scooter and sat for a moment, unable to look away from the Chapman guy. He turned then, his eyes finding hers. Again that rush of heat struck her. She shook her head. It was just the sun. She jammed her helmet on her head and started the scooter, heading toward the access road.

***

Rick saw her again. Wild and pretty, standing near a shiny little blue scooter. The girl from the sales office, Tammy, faded from his mind as he watched the plant angel ride away from the Institute. He'd hoped to stop there himself but the director hadn't had time to see him. Or so he was told. The director had time for her, though.

He ran his gaze over her and felt that stab of lust again. He couldn't really blame the guy. The little tree-hugger was something else.

The scooter was a dot in the distance as he finally got into his rental. The sales girl had asked him to join her for dinner, which he'd declined. *Never dip your pen in the company ink,* his father always said. Well, Tammy didn't work for Chapman Financial, but the advice was still worth something. Funny two of his father's ex-wives had worked for him before they worked under him.

He raked his fingers through his hair as he glanced in the rearview mirror. Hell, where had these waves come from? Damn humidity. He started the SUV and turned the AC on full, earning a blast of hot air in his face. He turned the wheel and steered the vehicle away from Cypress Corners and toward the beach. And temporary freedom.

He'd think about nothing but sun, surf and specs on the conservation development. Damn the weed. Damn the Institute.

And damn the hot little tree-hugger at the center of it all.

***

He sat in his hotel suite that night, his back to the ocean view. Even forty miles away from her, he was unable to get the plant babe out of his mind. She was the cause of all this, with her little notebook and her ugly plant. She probably had the director of the Institute in the back pocket of her snug little shorts. He pictured her again, as she'd been out at the site and across the street this afternoon. His body tightened.

He drained his beer bottle and began to peel the foil label into strips. Stopping, he laughed softly. Wasn't that a sign of sexual frustration? Well, he had that. Every time he pictured the little tree-hugger. He hadn't had such raging hormonal urges since high school. Maybe her frustrating his business plan was screwing around with the rest of him.

Sex was usually pretty easy for him, with no strings attached. He only got involved with women who had the same expectations. He suspected the plant girl wasn't like those women. Strings? Oh, yeah. Well, he wouldn't be the one getting tangled. Just look at the mess his father was in now.

Bill married Tiffany three months ago, and almost since the ceremony she'd been trying to get Rick into bed. Leaving suggestive messages on his voice mail, stopping by his office at Chapman for a quick chat about nothing. Low-cut blouse and high-cut skirt, blond hair as genuine as the tanning-bed cast to her skin. Tiffany was a bitch, but that was none of his business. Let the old man deal with her.

He stood, crossed to the mini-bar, and took out another five dollar bottle of beer. His cell rang as he twisted off the cap. Taking a long drag on the bottle, he grabbed the cell and held it to his ear. His father's voice came through clearly.

"Hello, Dad."

"Chapman," his father said. "I spoke to our guys in Legal and you have to get back to Cypress Corners."

He took another sip and settled onto the couch. "I plan to. The director of the Institute couldn't meet with me today, so I thought I'd give them a call in the morning and arrange a meet."

"No. Get back there and keep on those tree-huggers."

He stiffened. "Look, I can work just fine from here."

"You didn't work with them on the restaurant last year, Rick. You came in after I laid the groundwork. I made it easy for you."

His lips tightened as his father went on about how it was his conviction and balls that got the big job done last year. The café was just another step toward the next big project in the development, the lakeside recreation center. Bill wanted it and Rick had to make sure it happened. His mother's words came back to him. *You're as good as Bill Chapman, Ricky. You have to make him see that.*

"Okay," he said, cutting his father off in mid-diatribe. "I'll go back tomorrow."

"And check out of that hotel."

"What?" He sat up straight. "Why?"

"I want you to stay on the property. That girl in the office, Tammy, said she has the perfect place for you."

He blew out a breath. "Where?"

"A house for lease in the village. You can keep an eye on the Institute, maybe schmooze the Cypress Execs. Act like one of them. I didn't pay for all that schooling to let it go to waste."

He ignored the barb as usual. He had to hand it to Bill Chapman. The idea made sense. "All right, Dad. I'll get out there first thing."

"Good."

The call cut out and he was left holding nothing but air. Again. He had to go back, then. The plant girl was in tight at the Institute. She was the one who could turn this whole thing around, if he played this just right. He was smooth, thanks to the polish he'd gotten at the pricey schools Bill had paid for. He was smart, thanks to Harvard Business School. He was charming, if his success with the women in Boston was any indication.

He'd have to make up some ground. He'd been a clod out there at the site. No wonder she'd taken such an instant dislike to him. He'd acted like an ass.

He thought of how she'd eased his fire-ant bites, her delicate hands on his skin, her gorgeous eyes showing her concern and compassion. She was strong and gentle at the same time. A contradiction as well as a complication. The most compelling woman he'd met in years.

He smiled. Maybe staying in Cypress Corners wouldn't be such a hardship after all.

Chapter 3

The next morning Rick checked out of the hotel and headed back to Cypress Corners. He made a quick stop at the Sales Office. Tammy pressed a key into his hand and her breasts against his arm, but he ignored the calculated move. He wasn't going there. He thanked her and drove to the address she gave him.

All the houses in the development were charming and old-fashioned-looking, but he knew they were state-of-the-art modern at their guts. His temporary nest was a two-story deal, smooth stucco painted a soft gray and trimmed with white. A deep covered porch stretched across the front of the house, with two white rattan rockers sitting at the ready. It was all so neat and comfortable and Rick didn't really care for it. But it wasn't far from the golf course, and after he spoke to his father last night he'd called the Welcome Center and arranged a round with some of the Cypress executives.

He parked the SUV in the garage at the back of the house and carried his luggage and briefcase through the kitchen door. More hominess met him here. The interior was decorated with a country feel but without the flowers and baskets he'd expected. He found clean-lined furniture and buffed wood floors, leather couches and a widescreen TV. Cool.

A large basket filled with fruit, cheese and crackers sat on the kitchen counter. He read the card. A special welcome, signed by Tammy. Her cell phone number was hand-written below. He shook his head and took an apple from the basket, his mind on his coming meeting with the execs.

Yeah, they'd play golf. But more was at stake than strokes.

***

Harmony stepped out of the Institute later that morning. She'd taken plenty of pictures of the wild scrub buckwheat and uploaded them to the Institute's database, and now had nothing to do but think. Dr. Robbins had stunned her with his simple words of faith. He trusted her to keep the habitat secure. She was the one to keep Chapman's field man from infringing on the site. Well, she'd given her word. Her parents taught her to say only the things you feel are true. Pity that didn't always work both ways. That kind of honesty could leave you open to manipulation from those less truthful.

Ariel and Max Brooks had raised her among tofu and organic fruit, crystals and incense. Their small circle of friends were all the exposure she'd had to outsiders until she'd gone away to college. Everyone she'd known before was honest and upfront, which was the big reason Adam had so easily snowed both her and her parents.

He'd promised them a string of organic food stores to expand their own little shop, confusing them with investment-to-earnings and requests from fake investors. In a few short months their savings were gone and their dream dead and buried.

She still felt sick when she thought of what her parents went through because of her. Adam left her with nothing but guilt for getting her parents mixed up with such a snake. Oh, Adam had been more dangerous than a cottonmouth. The guy from Chapman probably hid the same slithery scales.

Well, she knew Dr. Robbins was authentic. He'd hired her while she was still in grad school and she wouldn't do anything to make him regret it. The position paid well and she'd make sure she earned every penny she owed her parents. If she had to go head to head with the guy from Chapman, she would. She'd protect the buckwheat and her job. She had to.

She turned and found him standing beside her scooter, dressed casually but looking just as starched in a navy golf shirt and khaki shorts. He did have nice legs. She'd seen that as she'd tended his ant bites.

She brought her gaze higher. His hair was curled from the humidity and made him look less menacing than he had at the work site yesterday. He smiled and her insides flipped.

"Hello," he said.

She nodded. "Hello."

He stepped toward her. "I want to apologize for yesterday. I was out of line."

"Yes, you were."

His smile widened, surprising her with the effect it had on his features. He looked much younger with that grin.

"You're not going to make this easy, are you?"

She felt her own lips curve. "All right. Say what you

want to say."

"I'm sorry… " He raised his brows in question.

"Harmony," she said. "Harmony Brooks."

"Harmony? Pretty name."

She liked the way his lovely mouth shaped the sounds. Her cheeks flushed hot. "Thank you. My parents are a little eccentric."

He chuckled and held out his hand. "Rick Chapman."

She took his hand. It was big and strong, the grip firm. Just as she'd expected. This was the hand of a man who went after what he wanted and usually got it.

"Nice to meet you, Rick. Wait." She withdrew her hand. "Chapman?"

He stared at her evenly. "Yeah. Of Chapman Financial."

"Oh, hell." She covered her mouth. "I didn't mean… "

He waved a hand. "It's all right. My father owns the company. I'm just the lackey who makes sure the money comes in on time."

The words were flip but she heard something odd in his tone. Maybe resignation, maybe resentment.

"It's nice to meet you, Rick."

"Likewise." He tilted his head toward the Institute. "I'm meeting with the director of the Institute this afternoon, but do you want to grab a bite to eat tonight?"

Her heartbeat skittered. Dinner? With him? He'd been so forceful yesterday, and taken with the attraction she felt today? No way. "I'm pretty busy."

"Oh, come on. Let me make it up to you." His gray eyes sparkled silver, like sunlight dancing across the lake. "I owe you for saving me from those ants. Twice."

She blinked. There was the charm to go along with those looks. It was an amazing thing to be the recipient of his attention. She thought for a moment, Hettie's words coming back to her. There were other things than plants to occupy her time, and where was the harm in one dinner? "Okay."

He smiled again. "You know this place. You pick the restaurant and I'll meet you in front of the Welcome Center. Seven o'clock okay?"

She nodded and watched as he turned and walked back toward the golf club. So she'd agreed to have dinner with him. Because of Hettie's comment? No, that wasn't the only reason. It was because he was the first guy to pique her interest in years. When he'd pinned her with those I-know-what-I-want eyes she couldn't resist. He was all charm and magnetism and determination.

Oh, she was still weak where his type was concerned. All she had to do was remember Adam to bring that point home. But this was only dinner. She'd keep her guard up and do her best to see to the task at hand. Staying informed of Chapman's plans could only help her keep her promise to the director.

She got on her scooter and thought for a moment. He wanted her to pick the restaurant, huh? She knew just the place to show Mr. Rick Chapman just what Cypress was about. The Boathouse.

Hettie waved from her usual table as she rode past, dropping a wink. That woman didn't miss a trick.

She smiled as she thought of The Boathouse. Mr. Charming Chapman would learn more about Cypress Corners than he bargained for.

***

That evening Rick drove his SUV to the Welcome Center. His golf game hadn't yielded any help with the

Institute, but he'd managed to shave a couple of strokes off his game. At least he had learned something from his meeting with the director. Through a special agreement, the Cypress developers couldn't infringe on any lands deemed protected. That included the café site right now, and the recreation center next year.

He had to get Harmony Brooks on his side. It was obvious the director held her in high esteem, if the glowing words he'd used to describe her knowledge and persistence was any indication. Rick could guess she had more power in those delicate hands than even she realized.

Keeping her close would give him information he couldn't get any other way, especially if the tree-huggers dragged their feet on the matter. Any delays could put their stake in the development in jeopardy. If it turned out that Chapman had to find another spot before the deadline, he could sure use her help. His father's words struck him. Time was money, all right. That was the only "time" Bill ever had for his kids.

Dinner with her wouldn't be a hardship. He bet she cleaned up nice, not that she wasn't fabulous flushed and rumpled from the heat, her hair wild as it escaped that ponytail. Harmony. The name was a little flaky but somehow it fit her. She seemed to blend right in with the nature around her out at the building site—her clothes, her skin, her hair. All green, tan and gold.

As he parked he saw her scooter sat out front and she stood waiting beside it. She wore shorts again, he was happy to see, with those little hiking boots, dressed up with a gauzy top. And her hair... It was loose and flowed down her back in silky curls. He shut off the engine and got out.

"Hello," he said as he walked over to her.

"Hello."

She lowered her eyes and he saw her lashes were thick and long. Was she blushing? No, she was probably just sun-kissed on her nose and cheeks. Man, her skin looked smooth.

"So where are we headed?" he asked.

She glanced up at him again. Now her eyes sparkled and she looked like she was holding back a laugh. "There's a great little restaurant on the other side of the lake, Mr. Chapman."

"Rick," he corrected.

She blinked those long lashes for a moment. "Rick,"

she said with a nod. "You can sample some of the local cuisine."

He deliberately ran his eyes over her. Oh, he'd like to sample something and soon. He tamped down his libido and held the passenger door open for her. She climbed up to settle on the wide leather seat and he stared at the curve of her leg for a moment before closing the door. She was a pretty tempting package, but he was always the one in control. No woman tempted him to do anything he didn't want them to, even if he let them believe it was their idea. He'd just focus on the game if he was to see to Chapman's concerns.

He got in, started the engine and headed toward the perimeter road. "Where to?"

"Just follow this road around the lake, Rick."

Damn but he liked the way she said his name. Clear like a bell with a touch of huskiness. He shifted in his seat. Suddenly the supple leather upholstery wasn't so comfortable. Jeez, they were only talking and his body reacted. He could smell her. A subtle blend of citrus and flowers, either perfume or the soap she'd used. The scent was light but potent. Man.

After about ten minutes she pointed out a turn-off to the right. They followed a winding road which led through the woody growth toward what looked like little more than a sprawling shack by the lakeside.

He stopped the SUV next to a rusty beat-up truck and turned to her. "Here?"

She nodded. "This is The Boathouse."

He eyed the building and its surroundings. A restaurant with a name like that in Boston would be pricey and surrounded by expensive yachts. This one boasted a lone dock to the rear with a few small boats tethered to it. But lights shone inside the shack and he could hear music on the warm air as he stepped out of the car. Before he could reach Harmony's door she opened it and jumped out. He waved her in front of him and locked the SUV with a click of his key chain while he followed her. Walking behind her wasn't a hardship, either. She had a sweet behind he could look at all night.

The Boathouse was loud and crowded and filled with wooden picnic tables. The hostess showed them to one near the wide screened windows and he sat on the bench across from Harmony. It felt like they were still outside; the chirps and croaks of whatever lived in the woods were loud through the screen and the air was still thick. The fans above did little to cool the place. A waitress stopped by the table and handed Harmony a menu.

Harmony paused and glanced at him. "Trust me?"

He felt a stab of guilt at her simple question. Yeah, he knew she had an agenda. But at least hers wasn't a hidden one like his. "Sure."

She smiled, a sly expression that did amazing things to her mouth. "We'll start with two of the specials," she told the waitress.

The waitress nodded. "And to drink?"

"A beer." Harmony raised her brows and looked at him.

He grinned. "Make that two."

She didn't say much as they waited for their food. Their beer was soon served, cold and frosty in the bottle, and he drank deeply. He didn't know what the special was, but the aromas filling the place made his stomach growl. Spices and salt and the smells of frying grease made his mouth water. Well that, and the girl sitting across from him.

"Do you come here a lot?" he asked.

"That sounds like a line."

He tilted his head. "A lame one."

She laughed softly. "Yes, I do. You haven't been here before?"

He shook his head. "No. Last year when The Clubhouse was built we stayed over at the beach. It was easier to grab a bite on the way out there."

Harmony nodded and drank some more of her beer. A drop of foam decorated the little indent on her upper lip and he pointed to his own. "You have a little… "

She touched her mouth and he swallowed a groan as she licked the foam off her finger. He shifted again. God, this bench was hard.

The food soon came, sparing him any more embarrassment over his extreme response to her mouth. The dish held pieces of meat that looked like chicken nuggets, batter-fried and served with a trio of sauces.

Harmony popped a piece into her mouth and chewed. "Mmm." She looked at him. "Aren't you going to try it?"

He watched her mouth again. Her lips were rosy in the dim light of the place, full and moist as she licked them.

He stabbed at the food with his fork and dipped it in the orange sauce. The sauce was good, like spicy marmalade. The chicken or whatever was terrific. It was kind of chewy but very moist and flavorful. He ate few more pieces as she watched him with a small smile.

"All right, I admit it," he said. "This is pretty good. Is it chicken?"

"Nope."

He stopped in mid-chew, a sense of foreboding coming over him. "What is it?"

"It's alligator."

He stared at her. "Alligator?" he asked around a mouthful of the stuff.

She nodded and he managed to swallow. She laughed as he drank deeply of his beer, a contagious, joyous sound. He laughed with her and wiped his mouth with a napkin.

"Alligator, huh?" he asked at last. "Well, at least it wasn't one those grasshoppers."

She laughed harder, reaching out to touch his hand. He looked at her fingers dancing over his flesh. She stilled and he stared into her hazel eyes. Her skin was flushed in the light from the stubby candle on the table, and her luscious lips parted. Laughing Harmony was even better looking than arguing Harmony.

She seemed to realize she was touching him and quickly withdrew. He felt a chill where her hand had been. They returned to their meal, the alligator bits followed by a big juicy burger she promised was local beef, and when she offered to order him dessert he didn't argue. He'd just made sure she tried hers first.

"So how long have you worked for the Institute?" he asked as they dug in.

She blinked at him, then shrugged. "I've worked for the Institute for nearly six months."

Brr. Her tone was chilly. He just nodded at her terse answer. He wouldn't push her tonight. Damn, but he was usually able to get whatever he wanted from a woman. Information, a kiss, a lay. Harmony Brooks wasn't like the women he dated in Boston. Nope. He was having the damnedest time maneuvering around her.

Some sort of berry tart followed for dessert. It wasn't fancy but very delicious. A lot like the girl across from him. He noticed she took pains to keep from touching him again, but that didn't stop him from feeling the pull between them.

They returned to the Welcome Center and this time she waited for him to come around and open her door. She stepped out and gasped, looking up at the sky. He followed her gaze, seeing a purple-blue sky filled with stars. Some were bright but others were mere twinkles on the canvas. There seemed to be thousands of them.

"I've never seen so many stars," he said.

"It's because of the lights," she said, her voice lowered as if in awe.

"The lights?"

"They're dark-sky lights," she said. "Special street lights that shine downward and don't throw up any light pollution. They're more expensive than conventional lighting but they let all the stars shine."

He nodded and continued to stare up at a sky filled with more stars than he'd ever seen. "It's worth it."

"Isn't it beautiful?"

He glanced at her then, at the starlight dancing over her hair, her skin. At the pleasure etched on her face as she drank in that night sky. "Yeah."

"I had a nice time tonight, Rick." She faced him.

"Thanks for dinner."

"My pleasure," he managed to say.

He stared at her, at those pretty lips, and let out a breath. Unable to resist he leaned forward, drawing her scent deep into his lungs. She gasped and he felt it to his soul. He was so close, he could almost taste her. He could feel the gentle puff of her breath on his face.

"Harmony… "

His lips barely brushed hers when she turned away and hurried to her scooter.

He straightened in response. "You're… you're riding back in the dark?"

"Yes." Her voice sounded a little shaky. "I have a light," she added, flicking on a small headlight. "I do it all the time." She started the quiet motor and put on her helmet. "Well."

Her eyes were on him, big and dark, and he longed to finish that kiss.

"Um, good night," she said.

"Yeah," he said. "Good night."

As she rode off he stood there in the starlight for a long moment. Cypress Corners was a contradiction. For that matter, so was Harmony Brooks.

He shook his head. What was the matter with him? She was just a diversion. A means to an end. He thought again about that almost-kiss.

A means to an end? Then why did tonight feel like a beginning?

Chapter 4

Four days later Harmony stared up at the draped ceiling above her bed, trying to think about anything but Rick Chapman as she began what would probably be another sleepless night. Well, sleepless save for the dreams involving the man in question. Darn Rick Chapman of Chapman Financial.

He was sharp and focused, despite his easy laughter and boyish smile. He'd looked so much younger that night, less driven than she'd ever seen him. The Florida climate will do that, wilt people's attitude along with their clothes. But she wouldn't think he was anything else but what he seemed: a smooth-talking corporate guy with one thing on his mind. That darn recreation café.

She recalled that flush of heat when she'd touched his hand at the restaurant. When he'd leaned close and stared into her eyes out under that blanket of stars. When he brushed that gorgeous mouth against hers. Well, maybe he had more than one thing on his mind.

A cool breeze danced over her skin, let in through open flaps set high on the gable ends of her tent-cabin. She closed her eyes and focused for one delicious minute on what it would be like to be kissed by Rick Chapman, to be held by his strong arms, touched all over by those big hands. She shivered and she knew it had nothing to do with the chill night air. She felt hot and cold and like her skin was a bit too tight. Oh, he was dangerous.

Sure, he'd been charming a few night ago. There was no denying that, even days after. But she couldn't forget that first encounter, when he'd said he'd speak with the Institute and get her fired. She couldn't afford to let her guard down. She needed this job. Her parents needed her to look after them. She had to stay focused. She had to keep Rick out of her mind.

She'd managed to keep herself busy out at her camp, putting off a ride to the Institute for fear of running into Rick. *Coward.* But there was only so much to occupy her out at her lake. She'd sunned and read and paddled her canoe. She'd gone over her photos and notes on the buckwheat before hiking through the far end of Cypress Corners. Even as vast as the property was, she couldn't think of a thing to keep her busy out here tomorrow.

She turned onto her side and shut her eyes. *Out, darn*

you! Oh, how would she get him out of her mind and out of her bed, if only in her dreams? After a few more minutes of trying to fall asleep, she threw off the sheets and sat up.

"That's that." She snapped on the light on the table beside the bed.

The thick rag rug her mother had made for her was soft and springy beneath her bare feet as she crossed to her dressing area. She pulled on her boots, grabbed her flashlight and went out to the lake. The sounds soothed her, loud here on the narrow dock that jutted out over the smooth water. She sat, drawing her knees to her chest as she stared out over the water. Slowly she waved the beam of light over the water's surface, seeing telltale signs of others as unable to sleep as she. Water spiders and frogs winked back at her, their eyes yellow and green as the light touched them. Then she saw them, red eyes that could only belong to an alligator. She set the light on the dock beside her. No swimming tonight, then. She was too tired anyway.

She closed her eyes, but even the breathing exercises her mother had taught her couldn't calm her tonight. She was a wreck. Over some guy who wouldn't look twice at her if she wasn't standing right in the way of his investors.

But when he'd almost kissed her? Her skin heated again at the memory.

With a grunt of frustration, she stood and stalked back into her cabin. She picked up her notes she'd taken on the wild buckwheat and settled on her bed again. Leaf size, color gradient, stem width… At last her precise notes doused any lingering want or confusion and she settled down for a few hours' sleep.

***

Rick pressed upward, his muscles trembling from the exertion. Sweat trickled into his eyes but he sucked in another breath and held his position. Blood pounded in his ears and his legs flexed. One… two… three… With a whoosh of breath, he slowly lowered his arms. The stacked weights behind his head groaned as he released the bar. He arched his back against the bench, easing the tug between his shoulder blades. An hour in the weight room of the fitness center and at last his body was beginning to forget about Harmony.

For the past four days he'd thought of little else but the pretty plant girl. He'd golfed and swam and jogged over every damn trail this place had and he still couldn't get her out of his mind. The director of the Institute finally deemed him worthy of another meet but Rick still hadn't learned anything of value. The fate of the scrubby plant was still under advisement and Chapman was spinning its wheels. More than once over these past four days his father had found it necessary to check up on him. It was obvious Bill was scrutinizing his every move. Terrific.

He sat up and grabbed the towel draped over the weight bench and rubbed it over his face. God, if it weren't for the promise he'd made his mother he'd blow off this job and do what he wanted to. He choked on a laugh. What the hell was that, anyway? It had been so long since he even thought about his own dreams and aspirations, he didn't even know what they were anymore.

Bill officially left the family when Rick was twelve, but it had been years earlier that the man separated himself from his family. Rick was the oldest, with Jake following behind by three years. The youngest and only girl, Cassie, was barely six years old when Bill left. Rick threw down the towel. At least Bill's support payments had visited regularly.

From the moment his parents' divorce was final his

mother had tried to make up for Bill's absence. Her insistence that Rick had to prove himself to Bill still echoed in his mind.

Well, maybe he'd done enough to prove himself. Top grades in high school, excellence at track, entrance into exclusive Boston College—none of it had brought anything but more money from his father. Rick hadn't thought about it at the time he was in school, but taking business courses and accounting should've been the first sign that he'd never break free of Bill Chapman. The job offer as field man wasn't the end as Rick saw it, either. He wanted the top position at Chapman. But more than that. He wanted his father to finally admit his firstborn was worth more than the money he made the company.

He stood and crossed to the leg press machine. He sat and moved the pin to just beyond his last weight limit. Why let his arms and chest have all the fun, right? Closing his eyes, he pressed and released over and over until his thighs screamed for mercy. With a soft grunt he let the weights settle. His whole body reverberated with a low no-pain-no-gain thrumming, and his mind finally focused on something other than his attraction to Harmony Brooks and his toadying to Bill Chapman.

For the last thirty minutes or so, at least.

***

Harmony returned to the Institute. Another lovely day, another solitary ride to the Village Center. Another quick conversation with Hettie. Thank goodness the woman didn't know about her dinner with Rick the other night. She wouldn't want to guess the open speculation Hettie would indulge in, in full hearing of anyone sitting in the crowded square.

When she walked into the lobby she smiled at Becky.

"Good morning, Becky," she said.

"Hi, Miss Brooks. The director's expecting you."

This surprised her. "He is?"

Becky nodded. "He couldn't reach you out at your camp so he's been hoping you'd stop by."

She felt a stab of guilt. She didn't think anyone would notice she'd put off the drive to the Institute for fear she'd run into Rick. Well, Hettie had chided her for keeping to her camp like a hermit, but then she always teased her about her solitude. But the director took note of it, too:? Well, there was nothing else to keep her from the Institute so here she was. She was late, apparently.

"Thanks," she said.

Before she could knock on his door, Dr. Robbins called out to her. "Come in, Harmony."

"I'm sorry, Dr. Robbins," she said. "I wasn't aware you needed me here."

He waved a hand. "Please don't worry, my dear. I just wanted to give you an update on our progress regarding the scrub buckwheat."

She nodded and quickly sat down across from him. "What's going on?"

"I've been in contact with the FDACS, and they're asking us to do more research."

The Florida Department of Agriculture and Consumer Services, through its Division of Forestry, oversaw the recovery of endangered and threatened plant species in Florida. Between committees and subcommittees, she knew the request could involve plenty of work for her. Good. She was more than up to the challenge, and more than ready for the diversion.

"What do they need?" she asked.

"Well, the Endangered Plant Advisory Council meets

within the month, Harmony. They want to rule on the plant at that meeting. So I need you to search all over the property for evidence of the scrub buckwheat."

"Certainly," she said. "Where would you like me to start?"

"Take a camera with you, and some sampling equipment. We need you to find out if the plant grows elsewhere on property."

She stilled. Chapman had to be behind this. Rick, specifically.

"So Chapman can build on their chosen spot, I take it?" she asked.

The director's lips thinned for a moment. "Yes. We work *with* the developers, my dear. They have to satisfy their investors or Cypress Corners would be forced to take environmental shortcuts. That's the last thing we want."

She nodded. Too many communities in Florida did little to preserve the wildlife their residents claim to value. Maybe Chapman Financial made it possible to take a more cautious approach, but with their constant scrutiny and interference their involvement was hard to take at times.

She looked up to find Dr. Robbins watching her. She

shifted in her seat and nodded for him to continue.

"Look for seeds or seedlings or anything else that can indicate the plant's growing," he said. "Maybe we can get it off the endangered list."

A thrill went through her. This would be even better than finding the plant in the first place! Chapman could have their precious café if she could find the plant thriving here at Cypress.

She came to her feet. "I'll get right on it, Dr. Robbins."

He stood as well. "Good. See Becky for an updated map of the development. We don't want to miss one corner."

She nodded. This was what she needed. A worthy diversion from Rick Chapman and a worthy cause for her talents. Humming to herself, she went out to the lobby.

As she rode her scooter past the fitness center Rick stepped right into her path. She skidded to a stop and braced her feet on the brick walk. He pulled back, his eyes wide.

"Whoa!" He grinned. "Hello, Harmony."

She shut off the scooter and removed her helmet.

"Sorry about that. I… My mind was… "

He took the towel off his shoulders and wiped his face. "I was just working out. Killer facilities."

She nodded, her eyes running over his body. He was sweaty and mussed and… Wow.

"Umm," she began. "Yes, I've heard they're quite good."

"You don't work out here?" It was his turn to run his gaze over her and she held herself still. "Well, you're doing something right."

"I canoe," she rushed out. "I hike."

Rick nodded, a lock of damp hair curing over his forehead. He waved a hand over his chest. "Sorry about… this. I was headed over to the swim center and thought I'd just hit the showers there."

His shoulders were wide, his strong arms shown to nice effect in his red sleeveless T-shirt. His silky black shorts draped low on his narrow hips and she couldn't look away from the sliver of pale flesh below his navel. What was wrong with her?

"You look fine," she choked out.

He studied her face for a moment and she prayed her

cheeks didn't look as red as they felt.

"Hey, wanna do dinner again?" he asked. That boyish grin teased his mouth again. "Only this time I get to pick the place."

She opened her mouth to accept, darn her lack of control. She took a breath. "No, I… "

"We can hit the beach, maybe?"

An hour in the car there and back? No stinkin' way. She'd never be able to sit that close to him for that long. He'd know she was attracted to him before the first mile-marker.

"Thank you, but no," she said.

He waited, for some excuse obviously, but she couldn't think of anything.   The sparkle went out of his silvery eyes and he lost his smile. He straightened his body and she could feel him pulling away. Good. She had to stay focused. He certainly didn't have tender feelings to be hurt by her refusal to eat with him, for goodness sake.

"All right," he said. He showed a smooth smile much different from his previous grin. "I guess I'll see you around, then."

She nodded and watched him walk toward the swim

center across the square. He rolled those broad shoulders and swung those strong legs and she should have felt nothing but relief that she'd effectively ended any association between the two of them. They were at odds, weren't they? On opposite sides of the issue? She had to keep her work for the Institute first in her mind and he had to press Chapman Financial's intentions. Well, sort of. He wasn't asking to bulldoze the buckwheat. Not really. He was seeing to his company's interests. She was seeing to the Institute's. If those interests were opposed there was nothing she could do about it.

For a fleeting moment she thought about what it would be like to throw caution to the wind, to take a moment to feel something other than duty and obligation. To the Institute and to her parents. To share a nice dinner with Rick, maybe a real kiss afterwards…

No. She had to stay focused.

She jammed her helmet back on and started the scooter. As she rode, her mind ran in circles.

Her life was fulfilling, despite anything Hettie said. She was doing work she loved. She was slowly repaying her parents. She was putting aside any foolish hopes and dreams that died when Adam broke her heart.

Rick Chapman had no place in her life or in her heart. He wasn't looking for anything more than idle occupation while the issue of the worksite was resolved. Let him find it with Tammy at the Welcome Center. She was more his type, Harmony was sure. Polished and perfect, cool and citified.

And if the thought of the two of them together made her almost miss the turn-off to her camp? That was surely a coincidence.

Chapter 5

Rick was at the fitness center again. Over the past week he'd tried to put Harmony out of his mind. No luck.

Work didn't do it. He was cooling his heels for the time being, dancing to the tune the Cypress Institute played for now. Cooling his heels and waiting for his father's daily call. Bill wouldn't be happy to hear that he had nothing to report today, either.

Play didn't do it. Swimming and golf only filled his time, not his mind. The fitness center was packed with guys, but a few women worked the machines in front of him. There was a nice view of the lush green trees and shrubs outside the wide windows. The women on the bikes and stair-steppers in front of those windows weren't bad, either. Tanned and smooth, fit and healthy. In spite of himself he pictured Harmony's form again. She hiked and biked and canoed, she'd said. Well, her body was better than the pampered women in front of him. Lush and natural and… real. What the hell was wrong with him?

She was just a pretty girl with plants on her mind. She was just different from the women in Boston, that was all.

He'd asked her to dinner again, a reasonable request which surprised him as it flew out of his mouth. She'd turned him down without hesitation. Just drove away on that funny little scooter of hers. Bouncing gently along as she hurried the hell away from him. He let the weights fall and grabbed up his towel.

A glance toward the mirrored wall showed him a mess. His hair was wet and stuck to his forehead in curls. Stubble darkened his cheeks. God, it was the same way he'd looked when he ran into Harmony last week. Big surprise she'd turned him down.

In Boston he'd never let himself be seen without being clean and pressed and perfect. Bill ran a tight ship, a fact he shared with anyone who'd listen. His son had to project the corporate image at all times. Well, he wasn't the golden boy today. No, today he looked tired and sweaty and frustrated. Well, he was all that.

November loomed and there was still nothing on the site location's status. The Institute was dragging its feet on picking an alternative site, as well. He felt like his skin was too tight. He itched to get out of Cypress Corners for a while. To drive out to the coast and sit by the ocean. To ignore the damn stars above his head as he sat on his too-cozy front porch. Special street lights, Harmony had said. Yeah, right. Special girl, but he didn't want to think about her under those stars. He could almost taste that near-kiss they'd shared.

He ended his workout session after about an hour. A steam, then. Maybe that would bake Harmony out of his mind. He left the weight room and turned down the corridor leading to the private steam rooms. He'd seen them before, each one a little larger than a shower stall with a built-in bench and a place to rest his bottle of water. He dug out his fitness center pass and ran it through the conveniently-located drink machine opposite the row of opaque steam room doors. The bottles held flavored water, infused with different plant extracts. He chose one with lavender—to help you relax, the label said—and turned to find a vacant room. One door swung open and a rosy and steamy Tammy stepped out wreathed in moist air.

"Rick!" She flicked a long wet strand of black hair over one bare shoulder. "If I'd known you were here I'd have waited for my steam."

He easily deflected her flirting today. It hadn't been

difficult the first time and grew easier the longer he stayed at Cypress Corners.

"Hello, Tammy," he said. "I just worked out and need a steam."

Her eyes glinted as she ran her gaze over him. "Pity. Doesn't it seem so odd that we Floridians take a steam when all we have to do is step outside."

He smiled. "When does it cool down around here?"

"You should be here in July, Rick." She pouted. "It's really not *so* bad, is it? Especially out by the lake?"

He shook his head. "The lake's too crowded for my taste. Families, kids."

Tammy shrugged and adjusted her towel, which showed more cleavage for the effort. "There's always the other lakeshore. The one we're developing next year."

He recalled seeing nothing more than a notation on the site map he'd been given. With the trouble the recreation café was causing him, he hadn't given more than a passing thought to next year's big project.

"I didn't think anyone was allowed out there," he said. "It's pretty primitive, right?"

"Not really. There's electricity and running water but

only one tent-cabin. That girl from the Institute lives out there."

His senses sharpened at the unexpected information. "Harmony?"

Tammy shrugged. "I guess that's her name. She has the place all to herself. For now."

His mind quickly processed Tammy's disclosure. Harmony lived out there alone? Well, no wonder riding her scooter at night didn't faze her. Man, that girl never ceased to surprise him. Maybe he'd take a ride out there—

"Rick?"

He glanced at Tammy to find her regarding him closely. "Hmm?"

She smiled. "I lost you there."

He ducked past her. "My steam awaits. See you later, Tammy."

He entered the first available steam room and peeled off his sticky shirt and shorts. Naked, he settled back on the contoured bench, draped his towel over his waist and closed his eyes. He went over what he'd learned from Tammy and what he'd guessed so far. Harmony lived alone, out by the far lake. She was capable and self-sufficient despite the fact that her name sounded a little flaky. She was intelligent, though her knowledge didn't seem to extend to finances and the bottom line like most of the women he'd dated. God, she was gorgeous. Quirky and spirited. He thought of that near-kiss again. What would she taste like?

He pictured her wrapped in just a towel, like Tammy had been. Her skin glistening with sweat, her citrus and floral scent coming off of her.

The room grew hotter and he let out a breath. Sweat trickled down his chest to pool in his navel before making its way to the towel. He had trouble breathing and drank some of the lavender water. It certainly didn't help him relax.

The rest of his body seemed to think blood was only needed in one part right now, the one under the damp towel. Thankfully each steam room was outfitted with a cool water spigot. He splashed some water on his face and cupped his hands to drink. It felt like ice compared to the air. To his skin. To his thoughts.

Maybe he'd ride out to Harmony's camp. He had to know how the Institute was progressing, right? He didn't need to see her flushed cheeks or her sparkling eyes. He didn't need to hear her husky voice or throaty laugh. No. He only needed to see the job finished and to get the hell out of Cypress Corners.

If the Institute wouldn't give the information up, maybe she would.

***

Why did she let him get to her?

Harmony pulled on a pair of boxers and a tank top as she readied for bed. She sat and ran a brush through her hair, trying to wind down after a busy day. She'd ridden over the property, but could find no other sign of the buckwheat. The developers called the Institute almost every day, which could only mean that Rick Chapman called the developers just as often.

Well, she could find them another darn place for their snack bar. But she had to take her time if she wanted to do the job right. Identifying other habitats for the buckwheat was her prime objective. Well, not the only one. She thought of Ariel and Max. A lot more was riding on this assignment than one endangered scrub buckwheat.

Adam and his slick words and sweet promises. She

cringed as she recalled how easily he'd gotten her into his bed. She'd been such a fool. What did she know back then? She'd been just a stupid girl with no real girlfriends to ask about the snake. Only after, when she was brokenhearted and her parents were just broke, had she realized what an idiot she'd been. Well, it was up to her to repay them. That goal wouldn't change. She couldn't let Rick get in her way.

The night they had dinner he'd been almost relaxed. He'd nearly lost that sharp city edge that clung to his pressed and perfect clothes. When they'd looked up at the stars, when he'd nearly kissed her... Oh, she had to stop thinking about him. He didn't matter. She certainly didn't matter to him.

He was here for his father, and he claimed to be just a lackey. His words had been tinged with sadness no matter the careless way he'd said that. Well, her parents might be quirky but they loved her. There was no question about that. But it seemed like Rick actually worked for his father, not with him. Maybe there was more there than she could guess. Maybe he wasn't the driven one.

She slipped her boots back on and left the cabin. It was a beautiful night, clear and damp with that hint of coolness that meant autumn was at last on its way. The animals around her—crickets, tree frogs and larger night creatures—sang into the moist air. She headed for the dock and sat on the edge. She felt no lure for swimming tonight, just a need to breath. To relax. To puzzle through one problem at a time and get Rick Chapman out of her mind.

Stretching out against the planking she arched her back and reached over her head. Tension pulled but she fought it, pressing until she began to feel her muscles lengthen. Her legs pulled downward, her rib cage opened and let in the fresh, fragrant air. She'd center her *chi*, as her parents had taught her. She trained her energy on regaining her own strength as she cleared her mind of everything but the breeze dancing over her flushed skin.

Breathing in slowly through her nose, she began to focus. Blowing softy out through her mouth, she urged the tension and confusion to leave her. Her mind fought, but soon wound its own circles. With each beat of her heart thoughts came to her.

Adam. Rick. The buckwheat. The Institute. Her parents. The money. Dr. Robbins. The money. Rick. Her parents. Rick. Rick. Rick. She gave up and let her mind focus on his easy grin, his deep eyes. His amazing body. Oh, what the heck.

"Mmm… " she murmured. "Rick."

***

Rick took the access road to Harmony's camp and parked his SUV where it dead-ended. The walk wasn't long to her place but the two bottles of beer he brought were sweaty by the time he reached it. The stars above his head lit the way, that and the moon glinting off the lake's surface. The property around this lakeshore was yet untamed. Spanish moss dripped off the canopy of trees overhead. He came to her tent-cabin, smaller than he'd envisioned, and knocked on the thin wooden door with his knuckles.

"Harmony?" he called.

No answer. He peered inside. It was austere, but with touches of hominess. A patchwork rug covered the floor and wind chimes hung in each corner, tinkling softly in the breeze coming through raised window flaps. A bed larger than the cot he'd expected was covered with a worn quilt, rumpled like she'd just gotten off of it. Her notes were spread on the small desk in one corner, pens and pencils scattered on the surface beneath the lone light left on. He sniffed the air. He recognized that smell. Flowers and earth and something more. That citrus smell that seemed to cling to Harmony's skin.

He stepped outside again and glanced around.

"Rick." The breeze seemed to carry his name.

He spun and looked toward the lake. Had he heard his name? Man, he was losing his mind. He supposed lack of sex would do that. He heard it again, soft and breathy. There was a figure on the dock. Slight and lithe. It hit him then. Like the scent in the cabin, it could only be Harmony.

The sand beneath his boots muffled his footsteps as he approached the dock. She didn't hear him, just kept reaching over her head and arching her body.

"Rick," he heard her sigh.

Her incredible hair covered the wood, shining in the moonlight. She wore boxers and the tiniest tank top, her breasts pressing against the ribbed fabric. He watched her chest fall, hearing a soft breathy sigh on the exhalation. Her eyes were closed, her lashes dark on her cheekbones. A smile curved her mouth as she breathed in through her nose, pressing those gorgeous breasts back toward the stars.

He'd suspected her body was nice when he'd seen her in her khaki shorts and a camp shirt. But seeing her now in those low-riding shorts and tiny tank top? Whoa.

Her shirt rode up to show a flat, sculpted belly begging to be touched. Her arms and shoulders were as lean and strong as her legs. Her skin glistened in the moonlight, so smooth he longed to stroke his fingers over every delectable inch he could see. And several he couldn't.

He got hard. He couldn't help but picture her moving beneath him and the lust he'd felt in the steam room came screaming back to him. He sucked in a breath with each of hers, counting to ten as he willed his body to grow as relaxed as hers obviously was. It wasn't working fast enough.

"Harmony," he said.

She jerked and sat up, flipping her hair over her shoulder as she turned toward him. He could feel her apprehension and held up his hand in a slight wave.

She blinked and then squinted in his direction. "Oh!" She seemed embarrassed as she fidgeted on her bottom. "Rick. For a second I thought... What are you doing here?"

He stepped closer, looking down at his feet to let her

collect herself. He'd been a jerk to intrude on her solitude. He wouldn't make her feel like he was some leering pervert now. He held back a smile. Okay, he'd leered a little.

"I heard you lived out here and thought I'd stop by." *Lame.* He held up the beer bottles. "You know. To have a drink and hear if the Institute had anything new." He managed to smooth his expression. "May I join you?"

He waited for her response, watching her face. If Harmony didn't completely buy it she didn't let on. When she blinked and inclined her head a notch, he knew he was in.

Chapter 6

Harmony folded her legs and sat cross-legged. She waved him over. "It's a beautiful night but I suppose I could use a cold drink."

He handed her one of the bottles and sat, his chinos stretching as he mimicked her position. Nice and comfortable, these pants. He rested a hand against the dock. It wasn't made of wood like he'd thought, but of some kind of recycled plastic planking. He'd seen benches and other things made of the stuff scattered throughout Cypress Corners. It was smooth against his palm. No wonder she didn't mind lying on it.

As he shifted his knee touched hers but he didn't pull away. He noticed she didn't, either. He wished he had shorts on, too. Even her knees were sexy.

He focused on the night air and the sweet scent of the girl beside him. He shifted again and drank deeply. Looking out at the lake instead of staring at her seemed to help the need now stretching his comfortable pants.

"Nice view."

His comment hung in the moist air.

"I don't know anything new, Rick," she said at last.

He shrugged away the tightness in his neck her words caused. "There's still time," he said, more to himself.

They sat quietly for a few minutes. The lake seemed to stretch on forever, black at the edges far on the other side. Like that night at the dockside restaurant, he heard all sorts of sounds from the woods around them. There was a splash to the left and he glanced at Harmony.

Her eyes sparkled for a moment as she sipped her beer. She lowered her bottle and smiled. "Gator."

He froze. He didn't get up and run, which made him feel pretty good. She didn't seem worried so he took his cue from her and drank more of his beer. "I hope he's not related to last week's dinner."

She laughed softly and he turned toward the lake again. Now was his chance. To get her on his side and push the Institute to make a decision. To set aside the lust and the unexpected comfort he felt being next to her and get her to work with him. He had to get the job done, and damn his own feelings for the girl standing in his way.

He turned and flashed his most charming smile. "Tell me about your work at the Institute."

She visibly stilled, then took a sip of her beer. "You want to know about my work?" She gazed out at the lake for a long moment. "Okay."

He watched her, seeing irritation and relief as she obviously resigned herself to the conversation. He'd stepped in it now. "Yeah. I admit I don't know much about conservation but there has to be a reason it means so much to you."

"I've always been drawn to nature. Ever since I was a little girl. I'm thrilled to be able to do my part to protect it." She shrugged and faced him again. "I work for Dr. Robbins, mostly."

He nodded. "Nice guy. A little vague, maybe."

"I know he seems absentminded to most but I know better. He has a big property to oversee," she said in his defense. "Cypress Corners sits on over ten thousand acres."

"I know. Only a piece of it is being developed." He smiled. "I read the stuff at the Welcome Center. Even took the tour."

"The tour? With Tammy?"

"Yeah."

"She's the expert at the Center. She seems so efficient

and… polished."

He blinked, then thought about the plastic sheen to Tammy's particular polish. "I guess."

Her brow furrowed and she ran a hand over that incredible hair. "I must look just fabulous right now."

Yeah, she did. But he doubted she'd believe him at the moment. He kept his mouth shut and ignored the moonlight catching in every wave and curl trailing down her back and shoulders.

She took a breath. "Cypress Corners is home to me now. It has been since I graduated."

He stared out at the lake as he drank his beer, his eyes scanning for something. Another splash came from the lakeshore and he started. She smiled and he shakily returned the expression.

"Once I got my Masters I didn't want to crowd back in with my parents in their RV," she added.

He puzzled over that for a moment.

Harmony smiled. "I know, it's a little off. Your family probably lives in a mansion."

He thought about Bill's monument to himself and stifled a shudder. "My father's house is pretty big." Big and cold.

"My parents are a little different," she said. "Their place is pretty mobile and she cooks at all hours of the day."

"She's a chef?"

"Sort of. She makes organic treats for her friends. She also sells them to gourmet shops near Orlando and on the coast."

"What are organic treats?"

"I know it sounds like an oxymoron," she said. "But my mother makes a tofu cheesecake that you'd swear came straight from New York."

He shook his head. "Alligator and tofu? Interesting."

"And turtle."

He laughed. "Yikes." He placed his empty bottle on the dock beside him. "Any brothers or sisters?"

She stilled again. "This conversation is getting a little personal, don't you think?"

He slanted her a look. "So?"

"Okay, I admit it's kind of nice. Sitting here in the near-dark, drinking beer and talking about something other than plants and conservation."

"Or specs or contracts," he added.

She nodded. "There's just me. Ariel and Max had me late in life."

"Tofu and alligator and you in an RV," he said. "Where did you go to school?"

"My mother taught me. An early home-schooler, I suppose. But I'll bet I learned more from her than most kids did in the classroom. My mother has a thing about crystals and auras. The healing properties of being in balance." She shrugged. "I guess that's pretty different from a New England education."

He looked down as he ran his hands over his thighs. Home schooled and living in a trailer. But the way her eyes softened when she talked about her parents, he didn't doubt her education beat the hell out of the cold prep schools he'd attended.

"Not a lot of home-schoolers in Boston when I was growing up," he said.

She tilted her head to one side as she brushed a thick curl over her shoulder. It was an unconscious motion and way sexier than Tammy's practiced moves that afternoon. The moonlight now danced over her silky skin, catching in the hollow of her throat, on her delicate collarbone. She stared at him, a question in her eyes.

"Did you say something?" he asked.

A smile came quickly. "I asked about your family."

He chose to take her question where he wanted to. "My brother Jake is off climbing mountains or jumping off bridges." Her brows raised and he grinned. "He's into extreme sports. He travels all over the world, setting up obstacle courses and other places you can push yourself, get your thrills and break your limbs. My little sister Cassie is off in Europe."

"Europe." She ran a finger over the neck of her beer bottle. "I've never been out of Florida. What's she doing there?"

He didn't want to guess what the wild girl was up to. Cassie was a handful and if Harmony hadn't read of her recent exploits in the tabloids he wasn't going to bring them up. "She's going to school, supposedly. I get a letter once in a while." Truth was, Cassie didn't seem to want to confide in her big brother. Maybe Jake had heard something.

Harmony nodded. She took both their bottles and set

them aside. "You miss her."

He did. Her and Jake. "Yeah. There's not a lot of time to get together."

"Just holidays, then," she said.

He shook his head. "No. Not even holidays."

She touched his hand and he realized his fist was clenched tight against his leg.He pulled back and shrugged. "Bill Chapman's not a warm and fuzzy kind of guy. We don't have a lot of family get-togethers."

"What about your mother?"

The question shouldn't have surprised him. She'd talked freely about her parents. But he must have revealed something of the hurt he still felt when he thought of his mother because Harmony leaned toward him, compassion in her hazel eyes. Damn it, he didn't want her pity. He sure as hell didn't want to talk about his parents.

The way Bill had left them, the sad woman his mother had become. But it was there, questions clear on Harmony's face, her lips parted to ask something else about him he wouldn't reveal. He stared at those lips. Then he kissed her.

She was as delicious as he'd expected, tasting of beer

and mint and fresh air. Her skin felt moist as he gently grasped her arms. Pressing forward, he gave her his tongue and let her taste him. She sighed and didn't pull away. His hands were on her back, up under her tiny shirt to touch her skin, as she touched his shoulders. Her fingers played over him, light and tentative and man, he wanted her.

His goal had been no more questions. No more thinking about his screwed-up family. In this instant that changed, shifted. The one thing he'd wanted when he first saw her pounded through him again. To taste her.

His mouth left hers and he kissed the hollow of her throat. Her pulse was as wild as his heartbeat. He could feel it against the tip of his tongue.

"Rick."

Her voice was soft, rich in the thick night air. It reached into him as her hands worked the buttons of his shirt. Turning, he pulled the shirt out of his pants and pulled her to him. Her breasts pressed against him and he groaned softly.

"Harmony." His voice was muffled through her hair. Man, he smelled that citrus scent again. He breathed in deeply.

In an instant she was beneath him, her fingers in his hair as he kissed her throat again. He closed his hands on her perfect breasts, stroking, kneading. She arched and he pushed her tank top up out of the way.

A quick glance at her face showed she wanted this contact, this connection. Kissing one breast, he braced his arms on the dock and pressed himself against her. One shapely leg curved around his waist, her skin hot and smooth against his. He could feel her heat through her shorts. Was she wearing panties? He trembled at the thought of just slipping a finger up under the hem and finding her wet. Finding her ready for him. Did he have a condom? The thought whispered to him.

"Rick," she breathed.

Yes! He had condoms in his wallet. She moved against him, close and tight until they moved together. Her boot struck softly against his butt as she began a rhythm that nearly sent him over the edge. Sweet Jesus she was just like he imagined. She wanted *him*.

Pulling back, he eased a hand beneath the waistband of her shorts.

In the next instant she sat up and edged away from

him. "Stop," she whispered.

He shook his head and tried to catch his breath. There was no blood in his brain but he was damned if it didn't sound like she'd said, "stop."

"What?" he rasped.

She tried to cover her breasts with the tiny top and he fisted his hands to keep from tearing it off of her. He could see the fabric clinging damply, her breasts begging for more of his touch. She stared at him, clenching her hands in her lap. "No. I... No."

A second ago she was hot for him, wet and ready and so sweet. "I don't get it," he murmured, as much to himself as to her.

She turned away, her shoulders set. "I'm sorry."

He sat up as his mind began to focus. She wasn't a tease. She hadn't lure him out to her camp to get him all hot and bothered. That had been his bright idea. Then why did he feel cheated?

"Sorry," he bit out. "You're sorry. We almost make love and—"

She whipped her head around to face him. "Make love?"

He welcomed the anger cutting through his sexual frustration. "What did you think, Harmony? I just wanted sex? That I came out here to screw you?"

She flinched, but her eyes flashed at him. "Didn't you? Drinking beer and asking about my job. Cozying up to me by getting me to talk about my family." She gave a little snort. "I almost fell for it."

He blew out a breath. "Don't deny you wanted me. Just ten seconds ago you almost came. I felt it."

She stood and grabbed up the beer bottles. For a second he thought she'd crack him over the head for that last bit of genius. But instead she turned and stalked away from him.

"Good night, Rick," she said.

He watched as she entered her cabin and slammed the door.

"You wanted me, Harmony," he called. "As much as I wanted you!"

He heard a muttered something, most likely a curse, but the door remained shut. He looked down at himself, his body still eager for something it wouldn't get tonight. It wouldn't be a curse that made sleep difficult tonight.

He squeezed his eyes shut. "Well, damn."

Chapter 7

Harmony wrapped her arms around her waist and closed her eyes. Every nerve tingled as she sought control. It was bad enough Rick had intruded on her centering exercise. Her space. Her thoughts, if she were completely honest. She'd been fantasizing about him just a moment before he'd shown up.

He was right, darn it. She wanted him. She wanted his kisses. His touch. Oh, and his body. She shivered as one last tremor racked her. Her whole body felt swollen and tight. True, she wasn't a virgin. But nothing she'd felt before had hinted at what she guessed Rick could give her. If she hurried she could get him right back where she wanted him.

"No way," she said. "Never gonna happen, my friend."

He was still out there. She could smell him, believe it or not. What the heck happened? One minute they were talking about family and the next he looked so lost and hurt she wanted nothing more than to hold him. To comfort him against whatever made him look so forlorn. The moment after that...

She hadn't expected that kiss. Or the hunger it awoke inside her. There hadn't been anyone since Adam and that had suited her just fine. Until now.

"Don't kid yourself," she grumbled. She poured some water from a pitcher onto a towel and patted her face. "One kiss from Rick and you were in heat."

She'd expected him to be practiced, skilled and distant as he tried to seduce her. But she hadn't thought he'd be so hot, so fierce. It called to something inside her. Something that frightened her more than giving her trust to a man. She feared she'd surrender her heart to feel that closeness again.

Her response shouldn't embarrassed her. Rick was hot and a wonderful kisser. His smell, his taste, did things to her she'd only imagined. Oh, it was just an organic reaction. Surely it had nothing to do with the compassion she'd felt when she'd asked about his mother. There was a story there, one he guarded closely. Who was she to press him on the subject?

A sound came from a distance, tires spinning on gravel as Rick's SUV barreled away from her lake. Good.

She'd keep to herself like she'd vowed before. Passion wouldn't cloud her mind. Oh, even she didn't buy that. Rick made her hotter than Adam could have hoped to all those years ago. And just look what a fool she'd been for him! She wouldn't risk everything for passion. Not again. She wouldn't risk her heart on a man who could keep his focus as she lost hers.

Rick's vulgarity should have shocked her but he was right. She'd accused him of coming out her expressly to get in her pants. It was obvious he'd come out seeking information on the Institute's progress.

He was right about her response, too. It wouldn't have taken but a touch for him to send her flying up to the starry sky. Ooh, those strong fingers…

She changed into her nightshirt and grabbed one of the bottles of essential oils she kept on the ledge beside her bed. Touching a drop to each wrist, she breathed in deeply, closing her eyes once more. The calming scent of lavender filled her senses as she climbed into bed. But her skin still felt flush, her pulse still raced. Her hand moved over her belly, to where she ached unfulfilled beneath her cotton panties. Just one touch. She fisted her hand and pounded it on the bed. Oh, but only one person's touch would do, not that she'd feel it tonight or any other night. Rick's.

Turning into her pillow, she let out a moan of frustration.

***

Rick stood inside the Welcome Center three days later, staring at the topographic table display of the sprawling development. He'd stopped by the Institute but the redhead at the desk said Dr. Robbins was busy. He'd told Harmony the guy was vague. Maybe he was sharper than Rick thought. He certainly handled both the developers and the environmentalists easily enough.

The Center's interior was painted in greens and decorated with photos of Cypress Corners. It was built like an estate home, plush and inviting with expensive wood trim and light fixtures. He had an eye for that stuff, since he'd been raised with his father's money in Boston. Again the contrast of pricey real estate surrounded by raw nature struck him.

He joined the other people standing around the table as the tour guide's voice droned on from a far corner. He caught bits of the presentation, aimed to draw people to the very contradictions Rick found so perplexing. A championship golf course and five-star restaurants bracketed by pristine lakes and a friggin' pet park, for Christ's sake.

He tuned out the guide and the chattering prospective residents and looked at the miniature layout of Cypress Corners on the table. He found the lakeshore park easily enough, and the street where the house he was staying in was located. But far on the other side of the table was the other large lake. No tiny houses dotted that area. Not even the tent-cabin he knew was there. He pictured the small camp, the narrow dock that jutted out onto the lake. If he set his mind to it he could see the figures tangled on that dock, so close to something he'd only imagined before.

Maybe he was lucky Harmony had pulled away. Hell, she hadn't pulled away. She pushed him away with her sudden coldness. Maybe she did him a favor. He doubted one coupling on a smooth wooden dock would ease his need for her. Hadn't he spent the nights since then wanting her?

"… many pleasures here at Cypress Corners," he heard the guide say.

Rick turned to watch the animated guide. The guy
was about twenty-five, one of those fresh-faced people who
were excited to be wherever they were. He extolled the
place's many virtues to a group of about eight people who
would never guess the pleasures Rick was thinking about
right now. Steamy nights spent surrounded by nature,
urging you to give in to your baser desires. He laughed to
himself. Somehow he didn't think Tammy ought to put that
in the brochure.

Well, he'd killed enough time. Might as well go back
to his comfortable rented house and watch that big screen.
Then in a couple of hours he could hit the five-star
restaurant for another lonely dinner. At least he wouldn't
have to eat alligator.

He nodded farewell to the girls working the
information desk and stepped outside. That's when he saw
Harmony across the street and looking happier than he'd
ever seen. She wasn't looking in his direction, obviously.
He heard her laugh, light and throaty, as she threw her arms
around a woman with long curly brown hair streaked with
gray. The woman wore clunky shoes and a gauzy purple
skirt that had sparkly things on it. He could hear the bells

on her wrists and ankles from where he stood. She had to be Harmony's mother. The balding beanpole who picked Harmony up and twirled her around could only be her father. What an odd pair to produce such a daughter. Well, he was nothing like Bill Chapman, right? At least he hoped not.

A wildly-painted RV sat parked near the curb, smaller than he'd envisioned. Harmony had shared that with her parents? No wonder her tent-cabin was sparsely furnished. The girl was probably used to doing with the bare minimum. He felt a pang of guilt as he recalled the stuff that had crammed his room growing up. Not from his mother, no. From Bill, in lieu of his time.

He took a breath and started across the street. Maybe he'd avoided her since that night on the dock. But his mother raised him to show the manners God gave him. What harm was there in a simple "hello?"

***

Harmony hugged her parents, happy as always to see them. She wouldn't focus on the RV, showing spots of rust beneath the gaily-colored paint job her father refreshed every couple of years. This year it sported a mural, towering cypress trees dripping with Spanish moss surrounding what could be her lake. She smothered the thought of what happened near the lake, the shame she still felt for trying to ignore what she'd done. She'd led Rick on, let him think she was ready. Heck, she'd practically taken the man's clothes off! If he never spoke to her again she wouldn't be surprised. But maybe she'd be a little relieved.

"How are you, dear?" her mother asked. She adjusted the round glasses perched on her nose. "We haven't heard from you in weeks."

She knew to interpret the question at face value. Her mother didn't use false guilt like the girls at college had complained about. No, there were no games in the Brooks family.

"I've been busy, Mom," she said. "There's a species of endangered plant on the property and I have to find more evidence of it."

Max Brooks grinned. "That's my girl. Give 'em hell."

Harmony hid her smile. Max was a radical looking for something to protest—though he'd missed being a conscientious objector to the Vietnam War by a couple of decades. She hugged him again, tugging on the short black ponytail at the nape of his neck.

"The developers work *with* us, Dad," she said.

Her father shrugged. "Then why do you seem so edgy?"

"Edgy?" She pulled back, fiddling with the hem of her shorts. "I've just been busy."

Her mother snorted. She grabbed Harmony's wrist and brought it to her nose. "Lavender." She released her. "No, you're not edgy."

Harmony waved her hand. "I've been having trouble sleeping."

Her mother's eyes, a blue-green that sometimes seemed out of focus, suddenly sharpened. Harmony knew that look. Her mother missed nothing. Harmony only prayed she didn't wear her frustration on her face.

"Something's going on," her mother said. She turned to Max. "Max, don't you think Harmony—?"

"Harmony!" Rick called.

Harmony nearly jumped at the sound. Oh, great. Just what she needed when her mother's radar was in overdrive. A visit from the very "something" that was keeping her up at night.

She turned as Rick crossed the street toward them. He looked casual today, inn a light blue golf shirt and camp shorts that suited him better than the creased clothes he'd been wearing. His hair wasn't perfect, either. It was curly and mussed. Oh, her stomach did that flip thing again.

He looked expectantly at her parents as he joined them on the brick walk. She watched him for any condescension as he ran his eyes over the RV. Nothing but mild interest was on his face, so he'd probably gaped his fill before he decided to join them.

"Hello, Rick," she said. At least her voice was even if her pulse wasn't. "Please meet my parents. Ariel and Max Brooks."

Rick shook Max's hand. "Rick Chapman. Pleasure to meet you, Mr. Brooks."

Max shook his head and smiled. "Call me 'Max.'"

"Max, then." He turned to her mother who stared at him with those too-sharp eyes. "Nice to meet you, Ariel."

Her mother's light laughter joined the jingle of the tiny bells encircling her wrist. "Very nice to meet you, Rick."

Her mother's eyes settled on Rick's face as she

gripped his hand. Uh-oh. Harmony silently prayed Ariel wouldn't offer him a crystal, or something for the indigestion he would get two weeks from now. Her mother had a way of putting people on edge with her little "forecasts." She didn't want to guess what Ariel saw in Rick's future.

Flames of embarrassment flooded Harmony's cheeks as she clearly envisioned the future that could happen if she was ever alone with Rick again. She closed her eyes. She prayed her mother wouldn't picture her and Rick naked together.

"You'll join us for dinner, Rick," Ariel said.

She remembered to breathe. Whew. That wasn't so bad.

"In December, I think," her mother went on.

Great.

Rick looked from one quirky parent to another, his brows drawn together. "Okay… "

Her mother tilted her head to one side. "A bit cloudy. You could use—"

"We always get rain storms in the afternoon," Harmony said quickly. The last thing she needed was Ariel reading Rick's aura there on the street.

"What about dinner tonight, then?" Max asked. "We can go to The Boathouse, maybe? Killer fried clams."

Her mother still held Rick's hand, so he gestured with his left. "Oh, I think I'll pass tonight." He winked at Harmony. God help her, he winked! "I don't know if I've recovered from the last time I ate there."

She smiled. "I don't think the alligator agreed with him, Dad."

Her father looked genuinely confused by that, a look Rick mirrored.

"Oh!" Her mother released his hand at last and hurried toward the RV. "I have something for you, Rick."

Harmony squeezed her eyes shut. Please. Not a charmed wedding ring or a tie clip that once belonged to Ralph Nadar, please. The metal door slammed and Harmony faced Rick, gauging his response. He seemed curious and wary, a condition his parents easily incited in strangers. She wondered at that wink. Was he putting on the charming corporate guy for her parents? Well, his efforts wouldn't win him the benefits that behavior in Boston might. Her parents had learned as much from Adam as she had. At least *she* was stronger now, darn it.

Ariel bustled back from the RV, a familiar beige square in her hand. "You can't turn down my cheesecake, Rick."

He glanced at Harmony and swallowed. "Tofu?"

Her mother handed him the package, which he took after only a slight hesitation.

"Of course," she said.

He held it gingerly as he nodded his head again. "Well, I'll let you have your visit." He turned to Harmony. "Enjoy your dinner."

He smiled and again that charm poured off of him as he walked away from them. She mentally patted herself on the back for surviving their first encounter since getting nearly-naked with him on the dock.

Her mother clicked her tongue. "He's unfocused, Harmony. His aura is cloudy."

"Don't worry about Rick's aura," she said. "He knows what he's doing."

Ariel's head shook emphatically, her earrings swaying. "No. He's at a crossroads. But he doesn't know it." She crossed her arms. "And he doesn't know what he wants."

Harmony thought about that night on the dock, of his kisses and caresses that almost made her give up the safety she'd guarded since Adam hurt her and her parents.

Rick's not the only one who doesn't know what he wants.

Chapter 8

Rick turned to watch as Harmony climbed up the
narrow steps and into the RV. Her parents followed behind
and he stared at the closed door. Ariel and Max Brooks
were nothing like his father's colleagues in Boston. They
were a little strange. But they were open and genuine too,
like his mother had been. Harmony's mother had creeped
him out a little. What was that about dinner in December?
When she'd held his hand she'd stared at him so long he
wondered if she could read his mind. Man, he hoped not.
Not with naked pictures of her daughter floating around in
there.

He got into his SUV and drove through the
development. Back at his rented house, he set the
questionable cheesecake down on the granite countertop
and stared at it. It looked okay, if a little pale. Graham
cracker crust, maybe. He sniffed it. Or wheat germ. He
turned his back on it and grabbed up the remote, flicking on
the TV. Golf was on. Again.

"There must be fifteen golf channels on satellite
here," he muttered.

Well, vacationing business men and retirees needed something to do when it rained too hard or was too friggin' hot to actually play. For himself, he could think of several indoor activities he'd prefer to watching TV.

He sat on the brown leather couch and put his feet on the coffee table. Glancing over his shoulder, he looked at the cheesecake again. What the hell?

He grabbed it and peeled off the wrap. He took a bite. It had an odd texture, a little bit gummy, but the taste… Not too bad. Probably made with real vanilla, too. He thought about the recreation café their investors were eagerly awaiting. Maybe something like this cake would go with the rain forest coffee they already served in The Clubhouse. He ate the rest of the dessert and licked his fingers.

"First alligator and now tofu." He threw away the wrapping. "It wasn't chateau Briand and tiramisu. But not half bad."

His stomach growled for something more. Five stars didn't draw him tonight. He ordered a pizza and sat back down, flipping through the channels until he found a rerun of a sitcom that still managed to make him laugh. A bunch of friends who were nothing like real people, sitting around drinking coffee. He smiled. No tofu cheesecake for this bunch. He studied the female stars of the show. One of the girls had hair the color of Harmony's, but not the thick curls. Another one had a nice rack, but he doubted her breasts were as soft and firm as Harmony's. The third girl's eyes were almost…

"Forget it," he said. He rubbed the heels of his hands over his eyes. "Harmony's damn near perfect."

The pizza arrived and he dug in. Hot and spicy, with pepperoni slices all over real cheese. Nice. As he chewed he thought about that afternoon again. When Harmony's parents invited him to dinner he almost accepted. But what would they talk about? He knew nothing about organic anything. The way they'd hugged and kissed their daughter told him they loved her. Their openness scared him almost as much as it made him jealous. He'd always wanted that. Ever since his mother died.

Even with Jake and Cassie he didn't feel free enough to hug and tease them. It seemed he'd picked up a bit of his father's cool detachment over the years. He nearly lost his appetite at that revelation. He closed the pizza box on the two remaining slices and slid it into the fridge.

Harmony had that openness, too. One look at her face and he knew what she was feeling. She was pissed off at him right now, that was for sure. He couldn't blame her. He'd been a jerk. But she still wanted him. He hadn't missed the interest in her eyes. He'd been crude that night on the dock, but he'd been right. By every sound, every touch, every taste he knew she wanted him. She still did. Would she ever admit it?

He grinned. "Only one way to find out."

If he had the chance to apologize for the other night, and maybe taste her again, he'd take it. What the hell? He'd eaten tofu cheesecake, hadn't he? He had nothing to lose by trying something new and different. And Harmony was both compared to the usual women he pursued.

The drive to her camp felt way too short tonight. He was on edge, his nerves humming as he parked the SUV. He was just horny, right? It couldn't be that he wanted to see her face in the moonlight. That he wanted to hear her laugh. Or smell her skin.

Like last time, she wasn't in the cabin. He looked for her on the dock, but she wasn't there either. Walking closer down the planks, he saw something there. A couple of somethings discarded in a pile. Oh, man. He recognized that tiny top, those worn shorts. A little pair of pink panties were off to the side, trimmed with lace. A feminine touch beneath her more serviceable wardrobe. He glimpsed another layer the girl kept hidden. String bikini panties. Strings. He'd wanted no strings attached. But these were his kind of strings.

He heard a splash and stepped to the edge of the dock. There she was. In the water. He glanced back at the little pile of clothes. Naked. He closed his eyes. She drove him wild fully clothed. He'd combust if he saw her naked. Wet. Her legs kicking, her arms reaching... He turned away.

"Harmony?" His voice didn't crack. Amazing.

She gasped. He wouldn't think about her covering those beautiful breasts with her hands, brushing that long wet hair over one creamy shoulder. He'd think about... she was in the lake!

"What are you doing in there?" he called down to her. "What about gators, for Christ's sake?"

She laughed. He felt a splash of water on his boots and he turned slightly. He couldn't help it. She grinned up at him and splashed again.

"I checked for gators, Rick," she said. "See, you shine a flashlight over the water and… Well, I know what to look for."

He looked over the lake, at the moonlight shining over the ripples, and shrugged. "I just came to… I wanted to apologize."

She held herself still in water that came to her shoulders, her hair floating around her as she looked up at him. "Apologize? No. You have nothing to apologize for."

"I would have said something this afternoon, but your parents— Wait. I have nothing to apologize for? Why?"

She apparently didn't want to explain, for she gave a shake of her head. "Come swim with me," she said. "This is so much better than the pool at the Swim Club."

He stood there, one boot wet and one dry stuck to the dock. "I… "

She splashed him again. "Come join me for a swim. You're not scared, are you?"

He was scared as hell, but not of anything in the water other than her. She was dangerous, all playful and sexy in the water. This was a whole other side of her and damn if he didn't want to play along.

"I hope the water's cold," he muttered.

"What?"

He stripped off his clothes in an instant. "Never mind."

He jumped in.

***

Harmony had watched him, eyed that gorgeous body as he stripped. Mmm. What was she was doing, flirting and leading him on? Oh, she knew all right. She wanted him to want her. Again. Like he had the other night. She wanted to be free to experience what they could be together.

She swam away from him and he followed her. They splashed and laughed and he reached out and grabbed her ankle.

"Hey!" She let him tug her back to him. "That's not fair."

He whooped in triumph, looking much younger now. Free, even. Her heart began to pound in rhythm to her body. Oh, this was *not* good. She pushed off his chest and kicked away. When she was safely out of arm's reach, she sank her toes into the soft sand on the bottom and smiled.

"Well?" she asked. "What do you think of my lake?"

Rick looked around and stood, the water coming up to his chest. What a chest! Muscled and wet, hair that swirled over tanned skin. Her pulse raced as he stepped closer.

"I like your lake," he said softly. He touched her shoulder and played with a strand of her hair. "It looks good on you."

He leaned closer and she kissed him. Why not? Kissing Rick was even better than she'd remembered. His tongue was on her throat, her neck. He nibbled on her ear.

"Harmony," he whispered.

He cupped her breast, stroked her, and she bit her lip. It felt so good. Lifting her by her waist, he closed his mouth over her breast. Pleasure shot through her and she leaned back, her hair trailing behind her in the water. His cheeks were rough and they teased her flesh. His tongue was magic, his lips amazing. His fingers, those long, strong fingers that knew what she wanted before she did.

"Oh!" She wrapped her legs around his waist as he teased her below the water. "Rick!"

"This was a great idea," he rasped as he nipped her skin. He let out a little growl, playful and sexy. "Back to nature."

She couldn't say a word, just let him rub those big hands over her backside as she pressed against his hard belly. The water churned around them and she felt him there. Right where she wanted him to be.

For an instant she thought he'd enter her, he was so hot and big and hard in the cool water. The friction and heat between them made her almost crazy. She shifted and lowered herself on him. His hands gripped her hips and he held her still.

"No," he said. She looked at him in question and he smiled. "Protection."

Oh! At least one of them was thinking straight.

He helped her up onto the dock and she turned as he joined her, edging closer with a wicked grin on his face. "You're wet, Harmony."

His words did as much to her as his fingers had. She was wet. Achy and hot. He slid a finger inside her as he brought his mouth to hers. It was like the past three days never happened. Like they'd taken up right where they'd left off that night. Yes! She wouldn't stop him tonight. She wouldn't push him away. She couldn't bear it if he left her again. She wanted him. Right here. Right now.

117

She kissed him, arching closer as he stroked her. Deep. Fast. Slow. Perfect. His thumb circled her and she let her legs fall apart. It felt so good.

His breath was harsh as he pulled away. "Are you sure?"

His eyes glittered in the dark and she knew he wanted this as much as she did. But he gave her the power to refuse. Her passion swelled at that realization. She wouldn't refuse. No stinkin' way. Not tonight.

She licked her lips and nodded. "I'm sure."

He kissed her hard. "Gimme a minute."

He reached for his shorts and went through the pockets. She watched as he put on a condom. *Oh, my.*

Spreading her legs wide, he eased into her. "God, yes… "

She couldn't speak, her breath gone. He pushed. All the way in. Deeper than she thought possible. Then out again. He caught her face with his hands and stared down at her as he began to move faster. Driving into her until she thought she'd burst.

"Rick," she moaned.

Stars behind her lids, moonlight pouring into her.

Here was everything she needed. She held on tight. In the next instant she climaxed, hard and fast and sweet as he held her. He joined her, letting out a shout as he came with a deep shudder.

Wrapped in his arms, she felt the tension slowly leave his body. He stroked her cheek but she couldn't look at him. Her body still tingled but her heart ached. Why did she suddenly feel like crying?

She felt scared. Scared of what she felt for him. Of what she could feel for him. Tears pricked at her eyes and she turned her face away as he tried to kiss her.

"What's the matter?" he whispered. "Did I do something wrong?"

"You know you didn't," she said. "It's just... Never mind."

He brought his face to hers and kissed her, tenderly. Like a lover. Why was she acting like such a fool? They'd had sex. Wonderful, heart-pounding sex. She didn't love him. Sometimes she didn't even like him. *Liar.*

"You're so beautiful, Harmony," he said in her ear. "And so sweet."

Those hands moved over her again, stroking and

teasing. His voice was low in her ear, his body hard against her.

She gave in to it and they made love again.

Chapter 9

Rick gazed down at her, worn out. She wrung him out. He grinned. Twice. That first time she'd been as tight as a virgin. But she knew how to move. Man, did she know how to move.

"Harmony." She wouldn't meet his gaze and he kissed her forehead. "That was… Mmm."

She moved away, just a couple of inches, but he felt it.

He braced his hands on the dock and lifted off of her. He thought about that cozy bed I her cabin. "Well, we can't stay out here all night."

That got a smile. She brushed a long wet strand of hair off her cheek. "I should get to bed."

"Bed." He rolled to his side and sat. "Sounds good."

She pulled away, damn it. Instead of laughing and falling into his arms, she pulled away. Fine. He'd play it her way.

"Rick, I… "

He grabbed his shorts and put them on. "Hey, it's late." He handed over her clothes and pulled on his boots.

121

"I'll let you get some sleep."

She kept her eyes down as she quickly dressed. "I haven't... It's been a long time."

That stilled him. He stared at her. "How long?"

She lifted her head. Was that a tear on her cheek? No. Not brave, spunky Harmony.

"Does it matter how long?" she asked.

Yes. He didn't want to think of anyone else with her. He shook his head. "No."He shrugged. "It's none of my business."

She grabbed his hand. "You have to understand. I haven't dated much. Not since college."

He suspected there was something else. Some jackass had hurt her. He couldn't ask her about it. He wasn't any good at this closeness stuff women seemed to want. That was why he never got involved with someone like Harmony. Someone who would want him to stay after the sex. Someone who could make him want to stay. He grunted an answer.

She slipped on her boots and wrapped her arms around her knees. "I know this doesn't mean much to you, but—"

"What?" He wouldn't get angry. Not tonight. He felt too damn good after he greatest sex he'd ever experienced. Twice. Maybe that was why his head was so cloudy. It couldn't be that it happened with Harmony. But it wasn't like she didn't matter at all.

"This meant something to me, Harmony," he said.

She gave a quick shake of her head and came to her feet. "Please don't say something you don't mean, Rick. I've heard it before."

"Wait." He stood. "Some jerk in college hurt you, I'm guessing. Well, I'm not him."

She seemed to weigh his words before giving an almost imperceptible nod. "No, you're not." She faced him. "And I'm not that girl anymore."

Neither one said anything for a long moment. He could hardly think, his body wanting her again. Forcing himself to relax, he stroked her cheek. "We don't have to talk about it."

She visibly relaxed. He picked up the rest of his clothes and followed her as she walked to the tent-cabin.

"Good night, Harmony," he said.

They kissed and he felt a connection. This was so

much more than sex. Their lips clung for a moment and he lifted his head.

"Good night," she said.

He stood out there in the dark as she flicked on a light inside. Against the canvas he could see her figure, that body that fit him like nobody else's. He walked to the SUV and threw the rest of his clothes on the seat.

"It's none of my business," he told himself.

He'd only wanted a diversion. He hadn't thought he'd find one to fill his mind after his body was satisfied. She didn't want tender words after, which should have been a relief. But he'd almost said it, something sappy that would make her melt. Or smack him in the face if by chance he'd read her wrong.

But there was more to Harmony. More than the fabulous sex and the electric connection. Way more than he'd bargained for. He shrugged into his shirt and started the engine. He'd get this job finished and get back to Boston. Then he wouldn't have to think about her.

Or the way he felt when he was with her.

***

Harmony stretched out on the bed the next morning,

her muscles aching. Rick was an incredible lover. She could still see him leaning over her, coming inside her. Would she see him again? Did she want to? She'd almost told him about Adam. Sheesh. That's just what every guy wants to hear about after he sleeps with a girl: the last guy who slept with the girl.

"Idiot." She rose and readied for her day. A yawn caught her by surprise and she laughed softly. "At least I didn't need lavender to sleep last night."

She left her camp and threw herself back into her work. She wouldn't think about Rick. About what he was doing. If he was thinking about her. As her day went on, it seemed he made it easy enough to avoid him. There was no sign of him in the village when she went to the Institute to upload photos and drop off some samples that afternoon.

On her way out of the lab she stopped in the reception area. "Is Dr. Robbins in?" she asked Becky. "I didn't see him."

The girl shook her head. "He had a meeting with the developers. I think it's about the new construction."

With Rick too, then. He'd keep on both the developers and the Institute to see to Chapman's interests.

Good. It served as a reminder of what he was here for. That wasn't for her.

"I left some notes in his inbox," Harmony said. "Tell him I stopped by?"

Becky nodded and Harmony left. The developers were probably leaning on Dr. Robbins. No doubt with Chapman Financial's encouragement. She'd just have to redouble her efforts and find more of the scrub buckwheat, that's all. That would solve everyone's problems and Rick could get back to work. Back to Boston. She tamped down the ache that thought gave her. It was sex. Just sex. He didn't want her love any more than Adam had. She wouldn't give it. No. She wouldn't feel that pain again.

On her way past the coffee shop she spied Hettie waving from her usual spot. She waved in answer, parked the scooter and walked toward the railing in front of her table.

"Hi, Hettie."

Hettie opened her mouth to speak then let out a low whistle. Her eyes sparkled. "Harmony, what have you been up to? Girl, you look like you—"

Harmony's gasp cut her off mid-sentence, thank

goodness. "Hettie, I don't know what you're talking about."

Hettie laughed gaily and threw up her hands. "I say it's about time."

Harmony's cheeks flamed as she looked around at the crowded tables. No one seemed to be paying them much attention at the moment, but if Hettie didn't cut it out...

She came closer to Hettie's table. "I'm a woman, Hettie. I'm single." She leaned in to whisper. "I can handle a fling if I choose to."

"A fling? Ha." Hettie pulled back, her eyes narrowed as if she suddenly noticed something. "Oh, it's like that."

Harmony's heart tripped. "Like what?"

"I've seen you with that handsome Chapman fella. Wouldn't mind handling him myself."

"Hettie!"

"Go on." Hettie waved a hand. "I won't tease you. Are you and he an item, then?"

Were they? "Not in the least."

Hettie reached out to place her hand over hers. All teasing was absent from her gaze. "Careful, girl. Where the body leads the heart sometimes follows."

"Oh, now you sound like my mother." She pulled her hand away, closing it in a fist to keep from trembling. "All cryptic warnings and clouded advice."

Hettie grinned. "Your mother is a smart cookie, Harmony. Maybe you should listen to her."

"What, about crossroads?"

"Hmm?"

"Oh, she said that Rick is at a crossroads. That I'm at one, too."

"I don't know anything about any crossroads, dear. But if she senses something. And I sense something… " She ended with a shrug.

"Oh, don't be silly." Harmony returned to her scooter and waved at Hettie. "See you soon."

Hettie just watched her, her eyes as piercing as her mother's ever could be. Harmony turned away and headed back to her camp.

Hettie was wrong. Her heart wouldn't follow her body anywhere. Rick was just a diversion. Was he using their attraction to distract as well? To get her to lower her guard where her work was concerned?

"Focus, Harmony," she chided herself. "Don't be a

fool again."

***

Poring over her notes that night, she knew she'd found more soil able to support the buckwheat. Excitement running through her, she reviewed the PH levels and density once again. The root patterns and leaf matter indicated the plant had grown in several places over the past few years. If this were true, and she had no reason to doubt the findings, she'd have proof that the plant wasn't endangered. That would do more than allow the recreation café's construction. It could change the plant's status.

She'd ride out first thing in the morning and take more photos. Compile a report. Do what she was paid to do. If the Endangered Plant Advisory Council saw this, she could make a difference and secure her job at Cypress Corners. Earn that money she put into an account for Ariel and Max every two weeks since starting this job.

Riding out past the golf course the next morning, she spotted a familiar figure. Standing out on the green, Rick leaned on his putter as he waited for one of the other players to putt. It was too late to turn around and escape. Not once he saw her, darn it. He raised his hand and she quickly waved. She wouldn't stop. Why engage him in small talk in front of the developers? *Concentrate, Harmony.* Don't think about how yummy he looked in those shorts. How long and lean his body looked in his relaxation. Get past the course and onto the other side of the property.

Her heart began to beat normally as she rounded The Clubhouse. Just past the Welcome Center she turned down the sandy path that wrapped around the lake. Of course she thought about that dinner with Rick, when she'd seen flashes of the charming, seductive man inside the corporate smoothness. She swiped at the beads of sweat on her upper lip. Seductive, all right. What they'd shared on her dock would stick in her memory for a long time to come.

Under the shade of a cypress, she popped the top of her water bottle and drank. It was November. She shouldn't be this hot. Or this tingly. Well, that had nothing to do with the weather. Just that man leaning gracefully on his golf club as she'd driven past. Just a wave of that hand that had moved over her body with skilled determination.

"Oh, boy," she muttered.

She switched the scooter on again and rode around to

a spot she hadn't yet checked. She'd avoided this side of the property until now, and it was lucky Dr. Robbins hadn't been in the last time she stopped by the Institute. She had no excuse for neglecting it. It wasn't far from the residential area where Tammy had put Rick. Separated by a copse of trees and protected from foot traffic, the area was still a little too close for her comfort. She couldn't tell the director she didn't want to risk seeing her... ? What was Rick, anyway? Her boyfriend? Ha, she didn't think so. Her lover? Did one time—okay, two times—make a man her lover?

Stopping the scooter not far from the edge of the rough road, she pulled off her helmet. Blowing a damp curl out of her face, she set the helmet on the handlebar and took her supplies out of the trunk. Digital camera, notebook, sample bags, a small spade.

"All right, then." She walked through the brush, her eyes scanning for the scraggly plant. "Where are you?"

This was good. Concentrate on finding the buckwheat and not on Rick. No more thinking about Rick, darn it. Find the darn plant. Let the developers get on with the café. Let Chapman get its money. Let Rick get back to Boston.

"Ow!" She slapped at her ankle. Fire ants! Son-of-a... "Watch where you're walking, Harmony. You're not some city girl who can't recognize the little buggers."

Fire ants. Of course they made her think of Rick again. Of that first day she'd met him at the work site.

Then she saw it. The plant she sought. The scrub buckwheat that was endangered and, all right, a little ugly. Taking out the camera, she snapped photos of it, and the others she soon found dotting the field.

She lowered the camera, a grin on her face. "Oh, you beautiful thing! Wait till Dr. Robbins sees these pictures."

She took sample leaves near the bottom of the plants, careful not to disturb the young sprouts, and stowed them in the scooter's trunk. Scribbling in her notebook, she recorded the findings. She hopped back on the scooter and followed the road further. More weeds appeared as she rode by. Wow. It grew all over the place!

Rick wasn't on her mind as she rounded the turn at the golf course on her way back to the Institute. Her parents' debts were. Dr. Robbins' faith in her was. She'd earned her pay today, and hopefully managed to get a plant off the endangered list.

"Score!" she shouted.

Still smiling, she parked in front of the Institute and ran right into Rick. All thought seemed to fall out of her head as she gazed up at him. So much for keeping her focus.

"Harmony." He ran his eyes over her as she pulled off her helmet.

She wouldn't fix her hair. Let it curl all over the stinkin' place. "Hi, Rick."

It was so strange to stand here on the brick walk, calmly talking to him when last time they were together they'd been naked.

"What are you up to?" he asked.

She walked around to the trunk. "Research."

He stared at her, one corner of his mouth lifting. "You're excited about something. Tell me you found something."

She couldn't help it. She let out a sound like a laugh and a sigh. "I did. I found the plant. The weed, you called it."

"Harmony, that was—"

She held up one hand. "It's all right. I know it's not

the prettiest thing out here."

His gray eyes ran over her again. "No."

She felt that familiar dip in her belly. Focus. "It's growing all over the place, Rick. Down near the path around the lake."

"Your lake?"

She ignored how cozy that sounded. "No. The main lake, not far from the second residential area."

He threw back his head and let out a whoop. "Hot damn! Harmony, this is great news."

She shook her head. "Not yet. I have to get this information to Dr. Robbins and he'll interpret it."

"But they can build, right? Tell me they can build."

His questions sobered her. Chapman Financial and it's interests. That was his focus. Okay, then. "If the plant isn't endangered, I don't see why not."

"Wait. Your discovery can help the plant, too."

"That's what I do, Rick." She closed the trunk lid with a loud click. "I care about the plants. I don't worry about construction or investors."

He reached for her but she took a step back. "I… I know your work is important to the developers."

"The developers," she repeated. "Yeah, I'm only thinking of the developers."

"Look. I didn't mean anything by it. I have interests here, too."

She brushed back her hair and nodded. "I know you do. I know where your interests lie. In your wallet."

He fisted his hands, something like pain flickering in his eyes for a moment. "That's not true." He looked her over, his gaze holding masculine appreciation now. "And I seem to recall your interests lying somewhere south of that gifted scientific brain of yours."

She flushed hot and looked down at her boots. "Some interests are better left denied."

He snorted. "That's not the message you sent the other night."

No. She'd been a fool to let her body dictate her actions. Well, today her actions were clear and focused on her work for the Institute.

Cramming her notes and stuff into a canvas bag, she stepped past him. "I have work to do."

He reached out and stopped her. He was so close she could smell that scent that was uniquely Rick. She looked at his face and read the hunger there. Then he kissed her, right there on the walk in the middle of the Village Center. After a brief hesitation of shock, she kissed him back. Their tongues touched and she felt her knees go as soft as the sand at the bottom of her lake.

He brought his mouth to the side of her neck. "Sweet and hot," he rasped. "Just like you."

She pulled back and looked up at him. "That wasn't fair," she whispered.

"'Fair' is negotiable." His voice was low, rough. Then he seemed to collect himself as he shrugged. "Everything is negotiable."

Just like that, a chill washed over her. She darted a look around, relieved to see that no one was staring at them. Thank goodness they were nowhere near the coffee shop. Hettie would never let her live this mistake down.

She straightened and fixed a glare at him. "And everything is a business deal to you."

With that, she went into the Institute. Thank goodness the walk was a short one. If she'd had to spend another minute in his sight she wouldn't have been able to keep her trembling hands from his view. His kiss!

Oh, she was a fool. There was no denying it now.

Chapter 10

A week and a half had passed since her encounter with Rick in front of the Institute, and Harmony managed to avoid his company for that stretch of time. She wouldn't dare find herself close to him again, not alone. Apparently she had as little control around him as she'd had around Adam. Renewed focus on her job, on her debt to her parents, was all she'd let drive her now.

After a quick tour of an untamed portion of the property, she arrived back at her camp to find a note tacked to the door of her cabin. She recognized the handwriting and a thrill of excitement struck her. It was from Dr. Robbins. She'd compiled and delivered her report on the scrub buckwheat to the Institute several days earlier, and knew the Advisory Council had met last night. She'd hardly slept, and for once in the past ten days it had nothing to do with Rick. Everything rode on the Council's decision. In her estimation anyway. She wiped her palms on her shorts and plucked the note from the door.

She tore it open and read the contents. Twice. Oh. She closed her eyes. Oh! The plant had been downgraded to threatened. She let out a whoop.

"*Eriogonum longifolium, var. gnaphali folium.*" She did a little twisty dance and waved the paper in the air. "Oh, you beautiful weed!"

She hurried into the cabin to change out of her dusty clothes. She had to get to the village. She had to see the documents for herself. She glanced at the note again and looked at her watch. Dr. Robbins wanted her to meet him at the Welcome Center in half an hour. She suddenly stood still.

"Rick." She'd have to tell Rick. Maybe Dr. Robbins would do it. He had to call the developers anyway, right? "Chicken lips," she chided herself.

She dressed and brushed her hair. Wearing her most capable outfit, khakis and a blouse that was more-or-less wrinkle-free, she got on her scooter and drove to the Welcome Center.

Hettie waved as she neared the coffee shop and she returned the gesture. "No time to stop today, Hettie!"

Hettie's brows raised but she nodded. "You best fill me in later, girl!"

Harmony grinned and nodded as she glided past. She

parked the scooter and stepped into the cool lobby of the Welcome Center. She saw Dr. Robbins right away, standing in front of the wall mural showing the development, past, present and future. The smile on his face made her grin in response.

"Harmony!" He turned to the two men beside him. "Mr. Forbes. Mr. Gottleib. This is Harmony Brooks."

Their presence brought her up short for a moment. She'd seen their photos in the Cypress literature, but had never been introduced. She managed to shake their hands. They were the top developers, the ones responsible for the whole project. She was surprised to find them dressed more like golf pros today than the heavy-hitters she knew they were. Old money and new, Forbes and Gottleib had put everything into Cypress Corners. She tamped down her unease and smiled.

"It's a pleasure to meet you," she said.

Mr. Forbes, a fifty-something man with a neat moustache and salt-and-pepper hair, smiled. "You're the girl who saved the buckwheat. Our heroine."

She shrugged. "Not so heroic, really. The plant was there, you know. I only found it."

"Nonsense, Harmony," Dr. Robbins said. "She's my go-to woman at the Institute. We couldn't get along without her."

She hid her surprise. Did they really think of her that way? She couldn't help but feel proud at the simple words.

"The investors will be pleased," Mr. Gottleib said. He ran a hand over his short flat top and smiled at Harmony. "Now we know who to call if there's another threat."

She weighed his words. A threat? To the development or to the environment? She wouldn't worry about that now. Not when Dr. Robbins was beaming at her.

"I'm glad I could help," she said. "I admit I was surprised I found so much of it growing on the property."

"I wasn't." the male voice stilled her. Rick.

She took a breath and turned, keeping her smile in place. "Hello."

"Rick," Mr. Forbes said. "How did Boston take the news?"

"Chapman is calling its investors as we speak," Rick said. "Now they'll easily find more money to put into Cypress Corners."

Mr. Gottleib laughed lightly. "Always happy to hear

that." He winked at Harmony. "Hard to find good golfing partners, too."

So he wanted Rick to visit in the future, Harmony assumed the man meant. She kept her face impassive. No one could guess her connection to Rick. Fleeting though it would prove to be.

Tammy slid up beside Rick, placing her hand on his arm and leaning close. She flashed a smile at the developers. "I can tell our prospective residents that we're on track, can't I Mr. Gottleib?"

Gottleib studied Tammy's cleavage for a full minute before nodding. "Sure thing."

Tammy turned to Harmony. "You're the one who found the plant. We're impressed."

Well, it was clear Tammy wasn't. The feeling was mutual. "Thank you." She nodded her head. "Mr. Gottleib. Mr. Forbes. Thank you again." She faced her mentor. "I'll catch up with you at the Institute, Dr. Robbins?"

"Of course, my dear," Dr. Robbins answered. "I should be there shortly."

She stepped out of the Welcome Center and stood for a moment on the wide porch. She wouldn't look back. She wouldn't go back in there and pull Tammy's acrylic nails away from Rick's arm. What did it matter? Chapman's interests were secured. Rick's work here was finished. It was best if she faced those facts.

She'd just ignore the twinge deep in her chest. And the secret hope that whispered he'd find another reason to stay.

***

When Harmony had brushed past Rick to make her exit he could smell her soft floral scent. It still lingered, even as Tammy still clung to his arm. He stepped aside to smoothly disengage her grip.

"If you'll excuse me." He shook the developers' hands and Dr. Robbins's. "I'll leave you all to your business."

"We'll see you later, Rick," Mr. Forbes said. "Maybe at The Clubhouse for drinks?"

He nodded an answer and left the Welcome Center. Harmony was just near the doors of the Institute as he crossed the street. He'd watched her from the moment she'd arrived at the Welcome Center, though she hadn't seen him. He'd seen the confidence in her stride as she'd joined Dr. Robbins. She'd held her own with the developers as well. Only when Tammy had joined them had he seen a slight change in her expression. If he didn't know her so well, if he hadn't fantasized about her gorgeous face for the past week and a half, he would have missed the annoyance on her face. A slight curve of her lip, a minute twitch of one brow as she studied Tammy's grip on his arm. So she'd missed him, too.

He called out her name but she didn't even turn around. She just slipped through the automatic doors and they slid shut behind her. He hurried across the street. The doors opened again with a whoosh and he stepped inside. The redhead behind the reception desk blinked at him. "Mr. Chapman?" She shuffled through the papers behind the counter and glanced at her computer screen. "Is Dr. Robbins expecting you?"

He flashed her an impatient smile. "No. I just spoke with him at the Welcome Center. Is Miss Brooks here?"

The girl grinned. She grinned like she knew about them. Harmony would not be happy if she saw the comprehension on the girl's face.

"She's in the lab," she said. "Do you need me to show

you the way?"

Hardly. He could probably find Harmony with his eyes closed by this point.

"No, thank you." He passed her desk and heard her humming softly to herself. He'd just ignore the possible implications of that.

He found the lab easily enough. It didn't smell like he would have thought, all antiseptic. It smelled clean and fresh, like they used some kind of environmentally-friendly cleaner. He shook his head. Of course they did. The room had rows of white laminate counters lined with thick-cushioned chairs. Computers sat along the windowed wall, the blinds drawn against the afternoon sun.

She was sitting in the back of the lab, her elbows resting on the counter as she stared at a small potted plant in front of her. He recognized the ugly plant. That weed with the long Latin name. The plant that had divided them then brought them together. Man, he could kiss the thing!

"Harmony."

She looked up and wiped at her eyes. "Hello again, Rick."

Her voice sounded odd, thick.

"Are you crying?" He stepped closer. "If it's about Tammy, there's nothing—"

She shook her head and grabbed a tissue from a box on the counter to blow her nose. "I'm not thinking about Tammy or any of the other women you've slept with."

"What? I haven't slept with—"

"I'm just amazed that Dr. Robbins and the developers have so much faith in me."

He sat and pulled his chair close to her, covering her hand with his. "I'm not." He stroked her arm. "I knew from the first day we met that you were dedicated to this project."

She tilted her head, that familiar sparkle in her eyes, and withdrew from his grasp. "What was your first clue?"

He grinned. "I'm thinking the fire ants."

Resting her chin in her hands, she laughed softly. "An auspicious meeting, I know."

He could feel the tension coming off of her, her shoulders held stiffly. Reaching out, he touched her again. "You've been under a lot of pressure, Harmony."

She started to object, finally nodding her head. "Yes. I haven't slept much lately."

Was that a reference to their night on the dock? He doubted it, not from the way her mouth drooped down slightly at the corners. There was more at work here.

He stood and put his hands on her back. "God, you're tense."

Rubbing his thumbs over the base of her neck, he felt her start to unkink a bit.

She leaned her head back and sighed. "Oh, that feels good."

He moved his thumbs down toward her spine and dug gently beneath her shoulder blades. "Relax. You're as tight as… " He couldn't finish the thought. He remembered how tight she was. Vividly.

When he kneaded her shoulders she let her head fall forward, her hair brushing over his hands. "So good."

Bending closer, he brushed the hair from her neck and kissed her there. "Yeah." He brought his mouth to hers. "Good."

Her lips parted beneath his and he leaned closer.

"Miss Brooks?"

He straightened as Harmony sat up. "Yes?"

The receptionist peeked into the lab. "I'm leaving. I'll

lock up."

"Wait!" Harmony called.

She started to stand but he placed his hand on her shoulders again. "She's gone." He turned her chair so she faced him. "We're all alone."

After a brief hesitation, he saw the heat in her eyes and brought his face to hers. She welcomed his kiss, reaching up to wrap her arms around his neck. He worked the little buttons of her blouse free and spread the material.

"I miss your little tank top," he said. "This lacy pink bra is a pretty consolation, though." He could see her breasts through the sheer fabric. He stroked his thumb over her breast and she gasped.

He nipped her through the bra and she held his head, her fingers digging softly into his scalp. "Rick."

He unhooked the thing and let it fall open, dropping kisses on her smooth belly. She leaned back and he worked her pants off of her. He kissed the skin just inside her right knee before draping her leg over an arm of the chair. Tiny panties, pink like her bra, didn't stand in his way. He touched her, slid a finger deep inside, and she shook. He put his mouth on her.

She tasted so sweet, hot and slick against his tongue as he made love to her. She stiffened but only for a second. She arched against his mouth and sighed his name. He stroked deeper, pressing her thighs apart until she straddled the chair. It rolled, smacking the table as he turned to keep them there.

"Rick," she cried. "Oh God, Rick!"

Shaking, she climaxed against his tongue. When she stilled he lifted his head to find her staring at him.

"I've never… " She looked away. "I know it sounds stupid, but—"

"Not stupid," he said. "Sweet. You're sweet. And I'm the first man to taste you."

She grabbed him and kissed him, her tongue arousing him as much as if she'd taken him into her mouth. She unbuttoned his shirt and stroked his skin, her hands working over his chest, his belly.

He switched places with her, settling into the chair and putting her on his lap.She still kissed him, her hair tangled in his hands as he stroked her back, her butt. She got his fly open. How, he couldn't say. But she touched him, stroking up and down until he thought he'd lose it. He had to be inside her. He had to feel her on him, over him. Just a quick second to put on a condom and he was there. He threw his head back and held on to her waist as she rode him.

"Yes!" she cried. His grip on her waist got tighter and he shuddered beneath her.

He held on to her as his mind slowly came back from wherever it went while they lost themselves. Her gorgeous eyes were cloudy as she gazed at him. Did he look like that, too? Loose and relaxed and more pleased than he could say?

"Man," he whispered. He held her close and she took his support and cuddled into him. "Harmony, that was—" His pants beeped. Frowning, he grabbed his BlackBerry out of his pocket and read the little screen. "Perfect timing, Bill," he muttered. He put the cell on the counter. "Let him get my voicemail."

He kissed her and sank into her heat again.

Chapter 11

"About damn time, Chapman."

Rick sat on the couch and closed his eyes. "I called you as soon as I got my voicemail, Dad."

It wasn't a total lie. He hadn't checked his phone until he and Harmony had finally worn each other out.

"I called the developers and they're satisfied," his father went on. "The contract should be fulfilled by the close to the deadline."

That was all true. Then why didn't Rick feel more gratified by that turn of events? "Looks like."

"I'll need you back in Boston after the first of the year," Bill said. "And Rick? I have a proposition for you."

His ears pricked up and he opened his eyes and straightened. His father hardly ever called him by his first name. "Go on."

He could almost see his father grinning. That should have put him on his guard but he was still pleasantly buzzed by his time with Harmony.

"If this project is complete by the deadline," Bill said, "I'll give it to you."

He must have heard him wrong.

"What?" he asked. "You'll give me what?"

"The top position," Bill said. "Under me, of course. I know you want it. You've been working hard. So if this deal goes through, you can have it."

The couch rocked beneath him. "Thanks."

"Well." Bill cleared his throat. "We'll talk sometime next week. Keep me posted."

He sat there as the line went dead. The top position. Executive Officer in Charge of Foreign and Domestic Investments. Man. He dropped the cell on the couch and rubbed his face. This was what he'd wanted for so long, tangible evidence that Bill believed he was worth something. He'd have it all: money, prestige and maybe his father's respect at last.

"Son-of-a-bitch," he whispered.

He had to focus if he wanted to prove himself. Opening up his laptop, he searched online for the companies he'd need to see the project finished. He'd handle staffing the place himself but he'd have to be careful picking the subcontractors and food suppliers. The place had to reflect Cypress Corners and its residents and visitors.

But the bottom line had to give Chapman investors the maximum return.

He couldn't afford to get sidetracked, to let his focus shift away from his sole purpose. He had to get the project finished and the investors satisfied. He couldn't get distracted. Nothing could get in his way.

His fingers froze on the keys. Harmony. Damn. He didn't have time for more than a diversion, right? That's what he'd told himself when he'd first stepped onto Cypress Corners property. She was more than a distraction. But she'd closed up after their first time together. All because some jerk probably hurt her. But now? After what they'd shared in the lab? She'd been soft and tender in his arms after. He'd never had a woman trust him like that, to show weakness after the pleasure.

"I won't have to stop seeing her," he told himself. "She isn't asking for moonlight and roses. Maybe just the occasional dinner. Definitely more incredible sex. This could work."

For now. Until he got back to Boston. He stood and crossed to the fridge to grab a soda.

Suddenly he had a bad taste in his mouth.

***

Harmony showered the next morning, letting the spray nearly run cold as she used up the reserve tank of hot water. Last night she'd been too tired, and too satisfied, to even think about doing more than falling into bed. Alone. She hadn't invited Rick over and he hadn't pressed her. But for the first time she hadn't enjoyed her solitude. As soon as she was dressed, she'd head over to the village. A stop at the Welcome Center to check on the rec café's progress would be interesting. A visit to the Institute was probably expected. Oh, she'd have to face Becky. She knew the girl had sent Rick to the lab to find her, and Becky could probably guess what happened after Rick innocently massaged Harmony's shoulders. Her skin flushed hot under the cool spray.

"No biggie," she said, trying to convince herself. "I'm a single woman. I can see whoever I want. No strings attached."

She rinsed the shampoo out of her hair. Yeah, right. She only hoped Dr. Robbins didn't find out about her and Rick in that chair. Oh, or on the counter. She flushed again.

The ride to the village seemed shorter today. She saw

Rick outside the Welcome Center, talking with Tammy.
Watching his body language compared to Tammy's, it was
obvious Rick wasn't encouraging her. She thought he'd
slept with her. Now she knew he hadn't. That made her feel
better than it should.

"Rick!" she called as she stopped her scooter.

He turned and waved a hand. Tammy nodded and
went into the Welcome Center as Rick talked to himself.
As Harmony got closer she saw he wore an earpiece and
fiddled with the BlackBerry clipped to his waist.

"Yeah, I know it's short notice," he said. "Listen,
those soda machines were promised. Before the delay." He
held up one finger and Harmony nodded. "I need them
installed by the fifteenth of December. The floor should be
finished by then."

He disconnected and smiled at her. "Sorry. I've got to
line everything up just right."

His eyes sparkled and energy poured off him.

"You love it," she said. "Admit it."

He grinned. "I do. After spinning my wheels for
weeks I can finally do something."

Okay. She wouldn't take that in the worst possible

way. "You'll get it done, I'm sure."

He opened his mouth when the cell beeped. Holding up his hand again, he turned away. "Next Thursday? Damn. Well it'll have to work, won't it? Get me the samples."

"Crackers," he muttered. He faced her again. "The flooring guys."

She nodded, ignoring his "cracker" remark. At least he hadn't called the guy a "red neck." Again the country girl felt out of place with the city boy. Just what had he thought of her "cracker" parents?

"Well," she said. "I was just going to check in with Dr. Robbins."

"Not in the lab, I hope." He winked. "He'd see that blush and know you were busy in there last night."

She wasn't used to the teasing. It was lighthearted and sexy at the same time.   She took her cue from him and shrugged. "I didn't get a lot of work done."

Rick grinned. "Hey, how about dinner tonight?"

"Okay," she said. "The Boathouse?"

"No way. I need to check out a place near Orlando. One of the vendors I'm considering supplies their desserts."

More of a work thing, then. Oh, well. A free meal and

good company? It worked for her. "Sure."

He kissed her, a quick press of his lips to hers that made her wish for more. But before she could lean closer his darn phone rang again. He tilted his head and checked the screen.

"I have to take this." He turned away. "Chapman here."

As he started talking about countertops and paint, she turned and crossed the street toward the Institute.

"Harmony, wait!"

She looked over her shoulder. "Yes?"

"I'll pick you up at seven."

Nodding, she continued. His voice was different on the phone, crisp and very Boston. Polished. Nothing like the soft words and throaty groans from yesterday.

"He has a job to do, Harmony," she told herself. "And so do you."

She entered the Institute, intent on losing herself in reports and data until the day passed and she could meet Rick for dinner. But which Rick would she see tonight? Warm, funny, sexy Rick? Or cold, driven Corporate Guy?

It turned out both guys showed up. Rick was dressed

in a sport jacket and tie yet looking as comfortable as when he wore shorts and a golf shirt. Boy, he looked yummy.

"We're eating at Lac des Fontaine," he said. "Lake of the Fountain."

French. She was sure it wouldn't be Creole. "Sounds nice."

"And expensive. But hey, Cypress people can afford to indulge, right?"

Most of them. "I guess."

They drove into the city, beautiful by city standards, but she still didn't care for it. The restaurant was situated on the shore of Lake Eola, facing the huge fountain set in the middle. The sky was pink through the wall of windows as the hostess led them to their table. The cool air was scented with burning candles and snatches of expensive perfume as they moved through the linen-dressed tables. Piano music tinkled in a far corner and she ran a hand over her dress.

She'd thought she'd dressed suitably, but when she saw the jackets and ties and expensive dresses she felt out of place in her batik-died shift. It *was* silk. It did look nice on her. Or so Rick had said as his eyes ran over her body.

"Here by the windows is fine," he said to the hostess.

The woman nodded and left them as Rick held out Harmony's chair. He lifted her hair away from the chair back and brushed her neck with his fingers.

"Get ready to enjoy some wonderful food," he said. "This place is better than   The Clubhouse in Cypress Corners."

She looked around at the cut crystal glasses and the forks lined up to her left. Suddenly she longed for the plank tables and fresh breezes of The Boathouse.

He ordered the wine and it was surprisingly delicious. Cool and crisp, like a fresh apple. After ordering in flawless French, he winked at her.

"Prep school," he said. "At least it didn't go to waste."

"Doesn't Chapman have investors around the world?"

He nodded and sipped his wine. "Yes. But I work on the domestic division."

There was something in his tone that told her he either didn't like that or that was about the change. Where would he go after this? She didn't want to think of him in Boston, let alone France. She put on a smile and held up her glass, glad to see her hand was steadier than her heart was beating.

"To Chapman," she said. "And to getting the job done."

He blinked at her then clinked his glass to hers. "To Harmony. For helping us get on with the job."

She took the praise for what it was worth. If she hadn't found the plant growing all over the place he wouldn't have been able to satisfy Chapman's investors. Money was the bottom line for Rick's company.

"Well, we both have our jobs to do," she said.

Rick nodded as he realigned the forks to his left. "Well, I'll be glad when this job is finished. Then I can get on to the next one."

She just stared at him. He'd leave, then. She'd known it all along. He didn't like it here. He'd made that clear from the beginning. As clear as the water in her lake. The lake. Swimming with him in the cool water. Making love with him on her dock.

Why had she slept with him? Because he was gorgeous and sexy and a wonderful lover, that's why. He made her feel things she'd only imagined before. Was

Hettie right? Would the physical lead to the emotional?

An even bigger question hung over her, clinging like Spanish moss and just as unshakable.

Why had she set her heart up for this hurt again?

Chapter 12

Rick nodded from across the table as he watched Harmony's gaze fall to her glass. He did have a job to do, but at least it wasn't coming between them anymore. Her plant was safe and her job secure. His position at Chapman was as well. At the end of the year it would all be settled. He'd be finished here and he could go back to Boston. Wasn't that what he wanted?

Their appetizer came, escargot in butter and wine sauce, and they ate. The delicacy slipped down his throat and he smiled.

"Snails," he said. "I guess that's as strange as eating alligator."

She returned his smile and ate. Delicately, like she did everything. She was as much a contradiction as Cypress Corners itself, pretty and tough and smart and sensitive. Man, did she look good in that little green dress. She wore strappy little sandals on her feet, showing off those lean legs. Her hair was loose and a little wild, like he liked it. As she sipped her wine he watched her lips. That mouth. God, it was as sweet and hot as the rest of her.

"So what's next for the Institute?" he asked.

She dabbed her lips with her napkin and shrugged. "More of the same, I guess. For me, anyway. More research, more investigations. My work didn't end with finding the scrub buckwheat."

Her words struck him. His work did. He knew it. She knew it.

"The developers seem pleased with the Institute's work," he said.

Her eyes lit up again. She leaned forward and placed her hands on the table. "Dr. Robbins has a unique position here. It's important to work with the developers. A property this size doesn't usually give more than passing notice to conservation. I'm just grateful I can do my part."

There was a conviction in her voice that he didn't feel with Chapman, and a loyalty to her boss he knew he'd never feel for Bill. He was always careful to never examine his own motives as he climbed the corporate ladder. Going for and capturing the next step in his quest for the ultimate job at Chapman, with no one above him but Bill. But the rewards were tangible, not like hers. The prizes were money and prestige, and that was all good. Recognition and respect. It was just what his mother had wanted for him. Just what he wanted for himself.

"You've proven yourself invaluable, Harmony. What's next?"

She looked puzzled. "Next? I don't understand."

"Next up for your career," he said. "What's the next position you're shooting for? A promotion? More money?"

She sat back, giving a shake of her head. "I'm happy with things the way they are, Rick. I'm making a difference and helping the Institute protect interests other than money. It's what I've always wanted."

Ouch. His ambitions were clear to her, then. Well, he didn't hide his ambition. It was a part of him, inherited from Bill and reinforced by his mother.

Thankfully their meals came and they could talk about tastes and textures as they ate the succulent seared tuna and filet mignon. He'd ordered dessert when they'd arrived, since the restaurant's signature soufflé took about forty-five minutes to prepare. But the pastries he'd consider for the rec café came on the heels of their dinners, arrayed on a silver platter dressed with paper doilies and powdered sugar. They looked almost too delicate to eat.

He lifted one to Harmony's mouth, the flaky pastry yielding as she took a bit. Whipped cream dotted her lip and he wiped it with is thumb. "Good?"

She closed her eyes and made a humming sound of satisfaction. He couldn't help thinking about the last time she made that sound. Her breasts in his hands, his mouth on hers as she purred beneath him.

"It's delicious," she said. "But too rich for me."

"Yeah, I guess it's too much for the café." He picked up his fork and cut the corner off another dessert, this one a square of key lime pie. He held it to her lips. "This one might work."

She licked her lips before taking a bit and he watched her react to the tart sweet filling. Her eyes widened slightly and she gasped.

"Ooh, this is the best key lime I've tasted," she said. "Mmm. Very refreshing."

Yeah. He swallowed. Refreshing. The soufflés arrived and the server poured white chocolate sauce over the steaming cake. Again he watched as Harmony ate.He could think of a few things to do with the decadent sauce, namely pouring it over her and licking it off her skin until she came

165

apart.

"Harmony."

She looked up, her lips parted. The smooth skin above the low neck of her dress turned pink as a blush spread over her. She was thinking about it too, he could tell. Her pupils dilated and she licked her lips. She wanted him. He'd had other women look at him with hunger. And maybe a dose of calculation. But this girl? Every expression was open and honest. Amazing.

He took out his credit card and waved it at the server. The hell with research for the friggin' café. He could only think of one thing right now. Her.

They rode back to Cypress Corners, Harmony sitting quietly beside him with her hands folded in her lap. She fiddled with the hem of that little green dress.Showing more of those smooth legs. Mmm. He managed to keep his eyes on the road until they were safely parked in back of his rented house.

***

"Oh." She straightened and looked around. "I thought you were taking me home."

He turned off the engine and pulled out the key. "I

166

did."

She looked away but again. She wouldn't ask him to take her back to her camp. No, she was… resigned? No, that wasn't the right word. She was anxious. Eager. She knew he'd make love to her again, with no promises. He would be finished with his job soon and would return to Boston. He'd probably never look back. But she'd remember their time together for the rest of her life. Why not add another glorious memory to that particular book? Goodness, she could certainly use those memories in the lonely years to come. It would be a long time before she ever let anyone as close to her as Rick was tonight.

Rick got out and opened her door. Anticipation seemed to hum through him as well as he urged her into the house ahead of him.

They walked into the kitchen and he removed his jacket, draping it over the back of a chair. "Some wine?" he asked.

She walked into the great room and stood beside the big leather couch, trailing her fingers over the back. "That would be fine." She pulled her hand away and dropped it to her side. "This house is quite lovely. I've never been inside any of the homes on this side of the development."

He poured their wine and put their glasses on the coffee table. "It kind of surprised me, too. I didn't expect it to be so comfortable."

She watched him, the muscles moving beneath his dress shirt, and felt the passion coming off of him. She wouldn't think about his words at dinner, his conviction that he'd leave soon and "get on to the next job." She'd just think about this, a passion and a wanting so sharp her breath was gone.

He turned and they tumbled onto the leather couch, sinking into the comfort and heat as he held her above him. She kissed him as his fingers moved up under her dress. Her panties were gone in an instant and his hands were there. His mouth was everywhere, on her lips, her cheek, her neck. She slipped the straps of her dress off her shoulders and closed her eyes. She wouldn't think anymore tonight. Let her mind worry about tomorrow. Her heart would feel tonight.

She opened her eyes and looked at him. Really looked. Yum. She pulled off his tie. She unbuttoned his shirt and eased it off his shoulders, all the while kissing him as he ran his hands over her back. His chest rose and fell as he moaned her name.

He cupped her bottom and she pressed against him. He was hard beneath her through his slacks and she undid his belt, his pants. Breathing heavy, he parted her legs and ground up against her.

"Yes," she gasped as he touched her there. Bracing her hands on his chest, she arched toward him as he closed his mouth over her breast. He sucked and licked until she thought she'd die from the pressure building inside her. This wildness... This was what they had for the short time he was here.

She lifted herself up and felt him enter her. Nothing came between them, just skin on skin as he thrust upwards.

"Harmony," he urged. "God, Harmony."

She rode him, leaning back to increase the friction. He was inside her, so deep she couldn't imagine where he stopped and she began. His hands were on her breasts, her hips. He picked up the pace, nearly arching off the couch as they matched tempo. The next second she climaxed, arching wildly as he exploded inside her. Legs trembling, heart racing, she collapsed against him.

His arms came around her, his hands soothing on her back as she regained her balance.

"Sorry," he said at last, his voice harsh in her ear. "No condom."

She lifted her head to regard him. The crooked grin on his face told her how sorry he wasn't.

"Should I worry?" she asked.

He brushed her cheek. "No. It's been a while for me. Before you, that is."

She had to take him at his word. He was a careful man, about business anyway. He took care of his body. She'd seen him after his workouts. So of course he'd take care of his health.

His brows raised. "Should I be worried?"

"About what?" He couldn't mean about her many lovers. Oh. *Baby* worried. She quickly did the calculations in her head. "No. I think we're safe."

He closed his eyes and held her close. "Good."

A pang struck her. Well, why wouldn't he be relieved? She didn't want a child any more than he planned on sticking around long enough to see it.

Then he was all smiles again, smooth and seductive

as he ran his hands over her back. "Stay the night?"

Oh, this was dangerous. She nibbled her lower lip. Here in his pretty little house, tucked next to him in what would probably be a huge bed? What the heck? "Okay."

He helped her off the couch. "I'll be more careful next time."

Next time? He'd make love to her again before the night was over. Her heart fluttered for a second and she caught her breath.

She was in trouble for sure.

***

Rick woke up next to her, her hair tickling his nose. The sheets were tangled around her legs, her fist was wedged in the hollow of his throat and she was snoring softly. He grinned. She was incredible.

Last night, when she'd set everything in motion downstairs, he'd been stunned. Aroused to the point of no return. He knew now what it felt like to be thoroughly fu-- No, that wasn't the word for it. She'd made love to him on that couch. He'd never felt that before, that connection. If he thought he'd sensed it the other times they were together, last night confirmed it. He was screwed, and he didn't mean physically.

Rubbing her cheek against his chest, Harmony sighed and snuggled closer. He waited for the familiar urge to flee, the burning need to sever any ties before they could form that always struck him the morning after. To his astonishment it didn't come. No "you've been great" or "about last night… " He wanted her there in his bed. He wanted to stay there all damn day, ordering food in when they were hungry and loving each other when they wanted more.

He stared up at the textured ceiling, trying to find the answers in the swirls of plaster. Nothing came to him. His mind was blank of everything but Harmony in his arms and liking it too much.

She lifted her head and yawned. Her eyes were slits beneath her curls and a smile curved her lips.

"Morning," he said.

Her cheeks turned pink. Man, she'd ridden him like a wild thing last night and waking up in his bed made her blush?

"Good morning," she whispered.

She ran her hand over his chest as she leaned away

from him and he felt it clear to his groin. He put his hand on her back and raised his head to kiss her. She kissed him back, but it was barely a brush of her lips.

He let her move away from him and watched as she wrapped her body with the thin blanket draped over the end of the bed, covering nearly every inch of that perfect body. Pity. She padded across the room and picked up the little green dress from where he'd thrown it last night. One sandal was in the corner of the room, the other on the tile floor of the master bath. Had he thrown it there? It didn't matter. He'd kissed her feet, the arches, the little toes. She'd wrapped those legs around him, up over his shoulders as he—

"I, um… " She fingered the blanket and bit her lower lip. "I have to get going."

So much for lying around all day, finding new ways to drive each other crazy. He watched her, looking so vulnerable with the blanket dragging the floor. Yeah, vulnerable. And a little frightened. Was she thinking of that jerk in college?

That made him sit up. "Let me get some clothes on."

She brushed her hair back from her face and nodded.

Throwing back the sheet, he swung his legs over the side of the bed and walked through the bathroom into the closet.

He wouldn't think about her hanging around all day. He'd focus on getting on with the day and leaving the pillow talk for the night. Tonight. Just as long as he got to wake up with her again tomorrow.

He threw on a golf shirt and a pair of shorts and when he came back into the bedroom she was dressed. Sort of. That dress was as thin as a scarf with the sunlight coming in the window behind her. Had she found her panties? Even he didn't remember where he'd left them. He closed his eyes for a moment. He wouldn't think about her sweet backside naked under that thin silk. No. He wouldn't.

"I'm ready," she said.

He drove her back to her camp. She didn't say anything, just stared out the window beside her as they drove over the gravel road.

"What are you up to today?" he asked.

She ran her hands over the wrinkles on the front of her dress. "I have to be at the Institute around noon."

"I'm meeting the developers at The Clubhouse at one," he said. "Do you want to join us?"

174

She turned toward him, her brows raised. "Today?"

Damn. Just what did that jerk do to her? "Did you think we'd spend the night together and I wouldn't want to see you again?"

She clicked her tongue. "Is that so unusual?"

He stared straight ahead for a moment, thinking of the one-night stands he'd had in the past. He couldn't think of one instance when he'd wanted to spend more time with any of those women, let alone another night together. "No," he admitted. "But last night was different."

Her eyes narrowed as they ran over his face. "'Different' how?"

He kept his expression neutral. Of course she wouldn't leave it alone. Research was her thing. Gather as many facts as possible before drawing any conclusions.

"I don't know," he answered honestly.

She didn't press him after that little bit of eloquence, but he could tell she wanted to. It wasn't that he expected a whole conversation about where they were going and what all this meant. It was more that she wanted to know but was holding herself back. Fine with him. He'd take the coward's way out and leave the conversation unspoken. He had no idea of the answers to those questions anyway.

A woman like Harmony would expect a man to love her. To tell her he'd stay. That's probably what that jerk in college had told her. Why else would she still feel that hurt?

Well, those words wouldn't come from him today. He didn't know what he felt for her, but he wouldn't say the words if he didn't feel them.

Chapter 13

Harmony sat and waited for words she doubted would ever come out of his mouth. There Adam and Rick were decidedly different. Adam was smooth and seemed to know what she wanted to hear before he even formed the words. She guessed Rick wasn't really cut out of precisely the same cloth after all. That was something, anyway. Well, facts and evidence, that was what she'd learned to rely on after Adam. Not her heart, that was for sure.

"Lunch at one," she said with a nod. "Sounds nice. I've never eaten in The Clubhouse."

He smiled. "It's no Lac des Fontaine, but I think you'll like it."

"I like The Boathouse, Rick." She shrugged. "I'm easy."

He grinned. "Not touching that one, sweetheart."

Sweetheart? She wouldn't read anything into the endearment. He was just being smooth and flirty.

He stopped at the end of the gravel road and put the SUV in park before turning toward her. She wanted to invite him in, to ask him to take a shower with her out in

177

the woods. To lay him down on that old quilt and let her have her way with him. But after their halted conversation? Not going to happen. Not today.

"Thanks, again," she said.

He grasped her arms and pulled her close, his touch gentle and commanding at the same time. "I had a great time, Harmony. Dinner and after dinner."

He kissed her and it was more like a branding on her heart than on her lips.   The next moment she escaped before she could say something really stupid. She didn't look back as she hurried into her tent-cabin.

Of course she heard the big engine race as he pulled away. She wasn't really listening for something else, hoping to hear his footsteps following close behind her. Nope. Not at all.

"Yeah, right," she muttered.

***

A few days after Thanksgiving, Rick showed up at Harmony's camp. She'd invited him to dinner with her parents for the holiday—organic vegetables and free-range turkey, no doubt—but he'd politely turned her down. Lunch at The Clubhouse two weeks ago, after that awkward conversation after their night together, had been nice despite the touch of tension. Ever since then the developers and everyone else at Cypress Corners acted like they were a couple. He wasn't sure how he felt about that. That bawdy old lady who sat in the Village Center, the one with the big hats and knowing smiles, had asked him about Harmony as if they were in each other's pockets.

Yeah, they went out. He smiled to himself. Yeah, they stayed in. The impressions they were apparently making with the Cypress folks were bad enough. He didn't want Harmony's parents thinking that they were more than casual. In his experience nothing could do that faster than a holiday dinner. His lip curled. Now he was here asking her to do something he wouldn't do in her place.

She never questioned his plans, holidays or long-range, and he made sure to never touch on the topic of what would happen after the rec café was complete. They hardly talked about the project at all, come to think of it. It was half-finished now, and on target for completion by the end of the year. That was just a few weeks away. Irritated as his thoughts threatened to linger on the subject, he stepped out of the SUV.

The late afternoon sun slanted through the tall trees behind her cabin and sparkled on the lake beyond the dock. He breathed in the pine scent and fresh air as he heard the water lapping against the pilings, the tension that had begun to plague him dissipated.

She had a pretty place here. He'd yet to spend the night though, listening to the things that chirped and splashed as he made love to her again. Surely that wasn't accidental. This was her place, and he really had no business hanging around through the night. He wouldn't press for that, either. Not after that awkward morning at his place.

He rapped on her door. "Harmony?"

He could hear her moving around, soft sounds as she straightened her home for his unexpected visit.

"Be right there!" she called.

Her footsteps must have been muffled by that thick rag rug because she startled him when she opened the door.

He'd surprised her too, apparently. She was dressed in low-riding pants with a hooded sweatshirt unzipped to show the tank top underneath. She had a pencil tucked up in the hair twisted at the top of her head, and she was barefoot.

"Were you working?" he asked.

She blew a loose curl out of her face. "Yes. But it's nothing that can't wait. What's up?"

Leaning a shoulder on the door, she appeared relaxed. But the uncertainty and tension hummed between them. It had since the morning she'd woken up in his bed.

He shoved his own preoccupation aside and forged ahead. "I need you."

She ran her eyes over him and he could guess what she interpreted from that statement. He would have taken her up on the offer if he thought she was as carefree about it as she appeared. But he needed her for something else today.

"Bill's here," he said.

She straightened, her eyes going round. "Your father? Oh, to check on the rec café."

"To check on me," he said too fast. "He brought Tiffany with him. My stepmother."

Harmony's brow furrowed but he wouldn't give her a chance to think of some excuse. "Come to dinner with us. Please."

"Oh, Rick." She stepped back and turned as he followed her into the cabin. "I don't know. The developers are fine but your father? Your mother?"

"Stepmother." He took her hand and turned her toward him. "I need you there, Harmony."

Her gaze searched his face for a long moment. God, he saw that tenderness in her eyes he'd seen off and on since that morning two weeks ago. He let himself bask in it for a long moment before setting it aside with a wink. "I can use the distraction."

That tenderness cleared, replaced by a conspiratorial expression. So she'd play it his way, apparently.

"Sure." She glanced down at herself. "Let me get dressed. We're not going to Orlando again, are we?"

"No. The Clubhouse." He stepped out held the door open. "Thanks, Harmony. I'll wait for you out here." He let the door close behind him.

***

Harmony dressed quickly. The Clubhouse. Casual elegance or some stuff like that. The little silk dress? No. A long gauzy skirt and matching top, both in sunny yellow. She'd look bright and cheery even if she was a bundle of nerves inside.

She was going to meet his father? His stepmother? Tiffany. Rick's voice had sounded bitter when he'd said her name. Something was up for sure. Rick seemed like he wanted to be anywhere else but with his parents. Well, he wouldn't explain why. He'd been Mr. Brush-off since they'd spent the night together. Keeping things casual, staying focused on his work and sleeping with her when the mood struck. But there were times, when he was deep inside her and gazing into her eyes, that she felt the connection he would probably deny. Her heart knew it, too.

Well, she wouldn't be the one to press him. She knew what he needed today and she'd be there for him. A diversion, a distraction. A buffer. She didn't know how valuable she'd be tonight but she'd sure try.

After putting on a little make-up and running the brush through her hair, she joined him in the SUV. She could sense the tension in him as he tapped his knee. Setting aside the implications it might infer—would he think she wanted more from their relationship?—she placed her hand over his. He eased instantly beneath her touch, and gave a jerky nod. He started the car and turned it around, heading toward the village.

She spotted the reason for his unease as soon as they pulled up in front of The Clubhouse. The two reasons, actually. Bill Chapman stood at the top step, one hand in his pocket as he sucked on a cigarette. Harmony said a silent prayer of thanks that the state of Florida didn't allow smoking in any of its restaurants or bars. The woman standing beside Bill seemed as harsh as the smoke coming out of her husband's mouth. Brassy blond hair framed a face that nature didn't make. Who has a nose like that, curved pertly at the end and tiny compared to her collagen-injected lips? Her body probably wasn't as God made it, either.

She swallowed the unfamiliar, unwarranted cattiness. This was Bill's wife, not Rick's girlfriend, she was meeting. Tiffany spied them and lifted a tanned arm and waved. About a dozen gold bracelets caught the light from the streetlamp.

"God, here we go," she heard Rick say under his breath. He faced her. "Thank you for this."

He seemed… smaller as he got out of the SUV and walked around to her side. He took her elbow as she climbed down and they joined his parents on the steps.

"Chapman!" Bill called. He threw his cigarette butt on the walk and shook Rick's hand. "Nice to see you. Who's this?"

He faced Harmony and she quickly looked him over. He looked a lot like Rick, only with hard eyes and a chill his son never showed. Well, hardly ever showed. Bill wore pleated tan slacks and a blue blazer over a white oxford shirt. The blazer had an emblem of a sailboat surrounded by fancy gold stitching. Some yacht club, she guessed. Small wonder Rick hadn't thought much of The Boathouse.

"Harmony Brooks," she said, extending her hand.

Bill took it and pulled slightly before dropping it. "Wait. The tree-hugger?" He turned to Rick. "You didn't tell me she was a knock-out."

Rick didn't say anything to that. Harmony faced his stepmother, who narrowed brown eyes on her. Curiosity mixed with blatant animosity struck her from beneath thickly-coated lashes.

"Harmony," she said. She pursed her peach-tinted lips and grabbed on to Rick's arm, leaning against him. "Rick didn't say he was dating anyone here."

Rick stepped back from Tiffany and urged Harmony into the restaurant. "Let's go inside."

Harmony wouldn't be hurt by his brusqueness. She knew it was due to these people and had nothing to do with their issues. Tonight, at least.

They followed the hostess to a table set in the middle of the restaurant. She didn't quite know why until the developers and other bigwigs at Cypress Corners began to stop by his table to say "hello."

"Great to see you here, Bill," one man said. "Your son here has done a terrific job pushing the end of the contract through."

Bill shrugged and sipped at his glass of scotch. "Rick's learning the ropes. He's proving himself."

She watched Rick, her heart aching. She'd never seen a family dynamic like this one. Tiffany devoured her stepson with her eyes—and her sharp fingernails as she used every excuse to touch his arm, his shoulder and probably his thigh, since she'd maneuvered her chair very close to his. Bill spoke only of investors and contracts. Rick didn't say much, just ate and kept checking his watch as he attempted to shake off Tiffany's hand.

The servers bent over backwards to serve Bill Chapman and party, and more courses than Harmony had anticipated covered their table. She picked at her food and waited for the evening to end.

"So what do you do, Harmony?" Tiffany asked after Rick's most recent rebuff of her touch. "Bill said you're the girl from the Institute?"

She set aside her napkin and nodded. "I'm a plant conservationist, Mrs. Chapman. I make sure nothing infringes on the native plants here on property."

"Plant conservation?" Tiffany tossed back her hair. "Sounds dull."

Rick cursed softly. "Harmony's work was integral to letting us build the rec café, Tiffany."

"Yeah. The weed." Bill waved his empty scotch glass at a passing waiter who whisked it out of his hand and replaced it with a full glass. "Rick told me about it when he first got here."

She wouldn't argue the point, not with these people. The thunder showing in Rick's eyes made her feel vindicated even though nothing either of them could say would convince Bill and Tiffany of her importance. She didn't care about their opinion. Just look how they treated Rick!

"How are Jake and Cassie?"

Bill snorted. "Your brother is off in… Tahiti, I think. Some extreme games, or something. Cassie?" He waved a hand. "According to the latest reports she's traipsing across Europe with some fortune-hunter."

"Reports?" Rick asked. "You're having her followed?"

Bill leveled a cold look at his son. "Better I hear of it than the tabloids. Your sister is out of control."

Harmony saw the pain flicker over Rick's face at the man's dismissal of both his siblings. She wanted to touch his hand as she'd done in the SUV, but once more Tiffany's bejeweled hand was there. And once more Rick pulled away.

At long last the evening was over and they all stepped out of the restaurant.

"I'll call you before we head back to Boston, Chapman," Bill said. "Tiffany wants to drive out to the beach tomorrow."

"Ooh, why don't you come with us, Rick?" Tiffany

said. Again she ran her eyes over Harmony. "You can bring your... friend."

"No." Rick practically dragged Harmony toward the SUV and opened her door for her to climb in. "Thanks, but no."

Tiffany shrugged one shoulder and pouted. "We'll see you in a few days, then."

Rick said nothing as he shut Harmony's door and walked around to the driver's seat. He said nothing and just sat very still until his father's rented convertible had driven out of Cypress Corners. Then he started the car.

"I'm sorry," he said, his voice devoid of emotion.

"Don't be," she said for lack of anything better.

He drove her back to her cabin. Resting his head on the steering wheel he was gripping tightly, he closed his eyes. "Why? Why do I let them get to me?"

She didn't hesitate. She reached out and touched his rigid shoulder. He softened a bit. "Do you want to talk about it?"

He lifted his head, his eyes red-rimmed. "It's always going to be like this." He laughed harshly. "Since it's always been like this, I shouldn't be surprised."

She grabbed his hand and tugged. "Come inside."

He followed behind her. A bit reluctantly by his plodding footsteps, but he followed. She knew he had to talk about it, to get it out. Her mother would cleanse his aura with crystals and get him feeling more like himself. Well, Harmony only had one thing to help him. Her feelings for him, whatever the heck they were. She only knew her heart was breaking to see him in such a state.

She'd worry about herself later.

Chapter 14

Harmony walked through her cozy cabin and flicked on the small bedside lamp. It's glow warmed the space but did nothing to the chill inside him.

"Sit down, Rick," she said softly.

He did so, folding his hands in his lap. She kicked off her sandals and settled next to him. His stomach still churned. What a hell of a night. He stared at the rag rug, tracing the patterns of colors in his mind as he tried to block out the memory of yet another awkward evening with his father and Tiffany, that bitch.

"I'm sorry I put you through that," he said. "I was selfish. I wanted you there as a buffer."

Harmony placed her hand on his shoulder again, like she had in the car. There was magic in that touch, something that had nothing to do with crystals or whatever her mother might employ. He leaned toward her, needing a compassionate touch. It was nothing like the moves his stepmother had made on him tonight, stroking him beneath the table while his father pontificated about something or other across from her. He'd been totally turned off, but it

191

had to hurt Harmony to see another woman act like she wasn't even sitting there on the other side of him.

"You have nothing to apologize for," she said. "I know they're your family, but… Well, they're not very nice people."

He blew out a breath and faced her. "That's putting it mildly."

She ran her fingers through his hair and he suddenly craved the contact. He stared into those soft hazel eyes, feeling the tension uncoil a bit inside of him.

"Tell me," she said. "Tell me why you let them treat you like that."

"Like what?"

She shook her head. "I won't touch what Tiffany was doing all night," she said. "That was wrong and a bit disgusting. But your father… " She seemed to be searching for the right word, and he was almost afraid to hear her opinion of Bill Chapman. "He treats you like an employee, Rick."

Wow. She was right. He'd always known it but to have her say it straight out like that punched him in the gut. He shrugged off his jacket and hung it on the bedpost. God, he felt like a fool. A fool and a lackey to his father. And now Harmony saw that as well. Nice.

"Bill Chapman made a place for me at his company, Harmony."

"But why do you work there? I know you've got the credentials to work anywhere. Dr. Robbins sang your praises to me almost from the start."

He looked down at the rug again. "I work there because... Ah, it's going to sound so lame."

She leaned closer, unwittingly giving him some of her strength. "Tell me, Rick. You can tell me anything."

He faced her, looked deep into those gorgeous eyes, and suddenly he knew he could tell her. "I do it for my mother."

She sat still as he told her all of it, of Bill's constant cheating and eventual abandonment. Of his throwing money instead of attention at him and Jake and Cassie. Of Rick's inevitable overachieving and his promise to his mother.

"That's it," he said at last, his voice harsh to his ears. He stretched out on her bed and folded his arms over his eyes. "Pitiful, huh?"

Harmony sniffed and laid down next to him. "No. God, no. Rick, you're amazing."

"Hardly." He wiped at his eyes and turned his head to her. "Tell me why your job is so important? I've never seen anyone as dedicated as you."

A smile tilted her mouth. "You'll think I'm making this up, but I do it for my parents."

This surprised him. "How do they figure into it? They seem pretty self-sufficient."

She nodded and fiddled with a button on his collar, the touch nervous but comforting as well. "They are. But because of me, they lost nearly everything. They were promised a string of organic food stores and sank all their money into Adam's… into the guy's scheme. I make good money here and pay nearly nothing in living expenses. I… I have to pay them back."

Ah. Adam. The jerk in college. "They were ripped off, right? By the guy who broke your heart?"

Lashes hid her eyes. "I never said Adam broke my heart."

He didn't know if he wanted to thank Adam for leaving her or flatten him for hurting her in the process.

"You didn't have to say it, sweetheart."

The endearment caused her to swallow. Well, he was sick of being so damn careful of everything he said to her. She was a sweetheart. She was his sweetheart and his lover and it was too damn bad if that jerk Adam had hurt her before.

He lifted her chin. "Look at me, Harmony. My story? Pitiful. Your story? Fine and good. Amazing, even." He kissed her, drawing her up against him. "You're amazing."

She held on to him as he began his seduction, apparently needing him as much as he needed her.

"There's more to you than you let on," she said softly.

Was there? He felt things deeper than he wanted her to know. Than he wanted anyone to know.

She kissed away the tears he hadn't wanted, her lips tender at the corners of his eyes. She stroked his shoulders as she held him closer.

"You're so much better than they are," she murmured. "You're a wonderful son."

He gave a tired shake of his head but she wouldn't let him pull away. Somehow he knew tonight would be different, at least for him. For her? He thought he could hear the emotion in her voice, feel the love in her touch. And just for tonight he needed it.

Coming over him, she unbuttoned his shirt and dropped kisses on his chest. He held her hair up off her neck as she moved lower, over his belly to his navel. She drew in the scent of him and he felt as if he were opening up from the inside.

He was prone beneath her, his breath catching with each kiss, each lick. Unbuckling his belt, she freed him from his boxer briefs and put her mouth on him. He moaned beneath her, moving against her as she kissed and teased him.

"Harmony… "

She seemed to act by instinct, mimicking those delicious things he did to her when he had her completely in his power. If she was a little awkward, a little tentative, it didn't matter. He was hot and hard and she licked every inch of him until he gently pulled her away.

"Not yet, baby." He brought her face up to his and kissed her. "Not yet."

He rolled her over and soon he had her naked beneath him, driving them both to an orgasm. Then he was deep inside her, his body showing her what he couldn't say as he drove into her again and again. She climaxed around him, her moans as sweet as her caresses as she held him close.

He poured into her, hoping the condom he'd put on at the last minute would hold. He'd never come this hard before, turning himself inside out as he shouted to the ceiling. She stared up at him after, her eyes shiny, and he almost lost it. He almost told her he loved her. Did he? Damned if he knew. But she was more than he'd thought a woman could be. She was… his.

"Ah, Harmony." He pulled out and she gave a delicate shiver. She turned into his shoulder and he held her. "Let me stay here tonight, baby." He kissed her temple, her ear. "Please?"

She looked him square in the eye then, determination mixing with the haze of passion there. "Stay. I want you here."

He closed his eyes and wished he could savor this feeling forever. This connection, this affection. It wouldn't last. But for tonight, he'd pretend he was just like everyone else, able to take love as it came and give it back without hesitation.

They slid under the thick quilt and loved each other again until she fell asleep spooned against him. Sweet and strong, his Harmony. Could this last?

God, he prayed he could find a way.

***

In the morning Rick kissed Harmony and she rubbed against him in her sleep. He stretched and reached for his watch. Damn. He had a meeting with one of the contractors this morning, in less than an hour.

"Harmony." He brushed her hair back from her face and kissed her again. "Baby, I have to go."

She stirred, nodding as she reached her arms over her head. The sheets skimmed her body and he thought about bagging the meeting. He couldn't. Bill was in town.

"I'll see you tonight," he said.

She nodded again and turned into the pillow. He threw on some clothes and drove to his house to get ready. His cell beeped and he clipped on the earpiece as he buckled his belt.

"Yes?" he asked.

It was the tile contractor, making some noise about delays and special orders.

"Look," Rick said. "I need that floor installed by the end of the week." He stepped over to the window, looking out over the manicured park and the wildness of the woods behind it. "Hey, bring a few more samples today. Maybe something… different. Stone. Something more natural."

The guy said something again in apology for the delay and promised to bring several tiles he had on hand. Rick thanked him and broke the connection.

He thought about Harmony's lake, and how the colors seemed richer out there. He picked up one of the booklets of paint swatches spilled on his counter and thumbed through it. Cool greens, warm golds and calm blues caught his eye.

"It could work," he said to himself.

The rec café was set in the nature walks, surrounded by Florida wilderness—well, tamed wilderness for residents and visitors to enjoy in small doses before paying big bucks for rain forest coffee and gourmet treats. Hmm.

He nodded to himself and switched on his cell again. If he had to meet Bill this afternoon, he'd better get on it.

For once he'd use Bill's influence to make some positive changes.

***

When Harmony woke up again Rick was gone. But by the clock on her night table she shouldn't be surprised. It was after eleven o'clock. The sheets still smelled like him and she turned her face into the pillow. Mmm. Her body still tingled from the memories of what they'd done. Well she couldn't stay in bed all day, reliving the most passionate night she'd ever known. But it had been more than that. For her, at least. She knew she loved Rick now. There had been no denying it after he'd spilled his story about his childhood, his ambitions. It had seemed different for Rick, too. It seemed he changed there in her bed. Opened up somehow as he gave her more than just his physical passion.

What a horrid man his father was. His stepmother? She wasn't touching Tiffany. She'd seen plenty of predators in Cypress Corners, and that woman was as vicious as any. She didn't know how Bill treated Rick's siblings, the brother who took dangerous risks for the fun of it or the sister who was doing something or other in Europe. Bill must have left his mark on them, too. Yeah, Harmony's parents were strange. But she never doubted they loved her. They never hesitated to show it, either.

Throwing back the quilt, she stretched and rose. She didn't have to go into the village until later today, and was surprised by the touch of disappointment she felt. She'd come to crave the connection to the people there, to Hettie and Dr. Robbins. Solitude wasn't all it was cracked up to be. Maybe next year, when her tent-cabin was a memory and her spot on the lake teemed with vacationers and residents, she'd find a house like Rick's in the village. She wouldn't need anything as large, of course. Maybe a little bungalow.

So today she'd review her notes until she had to go to the Institute, and work on the finishing touches to an upcoming presentation of the effects of birds' migratory patterns on seed distribution on property. As she tied her robe and gathered her things for her shower, she thought about that for a moment. It still surprised her that Florida birds flew further south to winter. The northern birds repopulated the area for just a short time. A thought struck her. Just like Rick.

He was here for only a few weeks, and eager to get back to Boston. Or even further away, as Chapman holdings spanned the globe. She wouldn't think about it, not today. His ambition would take him all over the world if he wanted it to. He made no promises and she wouldn't press him for any. Again she thought of the tenderness she'd seen last night. With a family like his, he was lucky he could feel anything at all.

That afternoon, she nibbled on a piece of tofu cheesecake. It was part of the care package Ariel had pressed on her after their Thanksgiving dinner, along with soy brownies and organic coconut chewies. She closed her eyes as she swallowed. Man, her mother could cook. Who needed those fancy desserts she'd tried in Orlando with Rick? She certainly didn't. He probably preferred them. He liked everything the Chapman money could buy. Again Bill's cold treatment struck her.

"Stop thinking about it, Harmony," she told herself. "Rick's a big boy. He'll probably never talk about his parents again." Or anything remotely related to his heart.

She wiped her fingers and opened a bottle of water. As she drank she heard a car skidding on the gravel road. Rick? She looked at her watch. No. He was probably still tied up with his father and Chapman business. She put the bottle back in her little fridge and peeked out the window. Her heart sank as she recognized the flashy convertible with the flashier woman behind the wheel. Tiffany Chapman.

Terrific.

Chapter 15

Harmony stepped out of the cabin and waited for Rick's stepmother to approach. Tiffany didn't hide her obvious distaste for the camp as she picked her way through the brush on high heels, tottering dangerously as one got caught on a root. For a secret moment Harmony wondered what Tiffany's reaction would be if she stumbled onto a fire ant mound. She swallowed a laugh.

"Hello, Mrs. Chapman." She closed the door and waited. "What can I do for you?"

Tiffany brushed her hair back from her face and adjusted oversized sunglasses on her tiny nose. "Harmony." She stepped over a log and ran her hands over her short blue skirt. "It's primitive out here. Backward."

"Yep," Harmony said. "Just me and the plants and birds. The wild animals."

Tiffany craned her neck and looked around at the woods. Then she shrugged and adjusted the jacket of her expensive-looking suit. "I don't know how you stand it. Rick told me it's got its perks, though."

That put Harmony on her guard. Had Rick talked to

Tiffany this morning? After he'd left her bed? No. He hated
Tiffany. Even if she hadn't seen it for herself last night over
dinner she'd have known it from the way Rick spoke of his
father and stepmother.

"I like it," she said.

Tiffany stepped closer and smiled as she removed her
sunglasses. She ran her eyes over Harmony and sniffed.
"You would."

Ouch. "What can I do for you, Mrs. Chapman?"

"I was just curious to see where Rick's little tree-
hugger lived."

"I'm not—"

"He told Bill all about you when he first got here,"
Tiffany cut in. "About how you and your stupid plant were
going to ruin Bill's deal."

This was interesting. Harmony crossed her arms and
leaned against the doorjamb. "And?"

Tiffany ran her painted fingers through her hair. "Bill
told him to take care of you, that's all."

Her heart began to pound and she straightened away
from the door. "What?"

"Bill told Rick to take care of the little tree-hugger.

To keep you busy until the Institute picked a new spot."

No. Rick didn't sleep with her to get her on his side. No!

Tiffany bent down and peered through the window. "How cozy." She straightened and winked. "I guess he did his job." She waved her hand. "And now he can finish Chapman's."

She couldn't speak. Could what this woman said be true?

"Well, with a closer look I guess your place isn't so bad," Tiffany said. "Looks like you have a shower out back. Hmm." She slid an ugly grin at Harmony. "No wonder Rick said roughing it wasn't a hardship."

"But he never... ," Harmony said to herself. "He—"

"He wants the top position at Chapman, honey," Tiffany said. "And he's willing to do anything for it."

Cold settled in her belly. No. Rick couldn't be like that!

"I don't believe you," Harmony said on a breath.

Tiffany began to pick her way back toward the car. "Believe what you want. Rick is Bill Chapman's son. Believe me, he has Bill's ambition."

She vaguely heard Tiffany start the car and drive away. Her stomach began to churn. No. Rick hadn't used her that way. They had a connection. She'd felt it in his touch. Seen it in his eyes. The truth smacked her square in the face. She'd fallen for it all over again.

"Stupid, stupid girl," she told herself. "You saw what you wanted to see."

Rick was just like Adam. Just using her to further his own agenda. She shouldn't be surprised. She'd known about Rick's ambition before Tiffany made it even clearer. It was why he worked at Chapman, why he took Bill's coldness and indifference for a chance to climb the corporate ladder and prove himself.

She sank down on the step, curling into herself as tears burned her eyes. She'd given Rick her body. That had been ridiculously easy. She'd given Rick her heart. Now that had taken some doing. He took all she gave as a corporate perk?

How could she be so stupid?

***

That evening, after a long day of work at the Institute, she packed up her things and headed out. She and Dr.

Robbins were finished for the day, a little later than usual but it had been a relief to lose herself in work. After Mrs. Chapman's lovely disclosure, it had taken some time to collect herself before riding into the village. But she'd given Dr. Robbins her full attention as they wrapped up the presentation. Thankfully the man only asked her what was wrong once before poring over their work again.

Rick had called a few times during the day, but she'd let Becky know from the first phone call that she didn't want to speak to him. She couldn't think of an excuse to tell the girl. She just wasn't good at lying. Her lip curled at that realization. That was her fatal flaw. Especially when seemed to she attract liars. Apparently it took one to know one, and she was woefully clueless in that regard.

She expected Rick wanted see her tonight. Why should she be surprised? Why shouldn't he want to take what she gave him until he left for Boston, right? Well, there was no way she could see him and not think about everything Tiffany had said. His career. His screwed-up family. His ambition. Her stomach couldn't take it. As for her heart? Her heart ached. She shoved her notes into her pack and opened the trunk of her scooter.

"Harmony!"

She turned in response to the familiar voice despite her resolve. Her shoulders slumped. Oh, great. Rick walked toward her, a smile on his face. Oh, he was beautiful. So big and capable. His smile did things to her insides as easily as those lips did stuff to her outsides.

"Hi, Rick."

He stopped in front of her, slowly losing his smile. "What's wrong?"

He saw too much, that was one thing. She wouldn't wear her foolish heart on her sleeve, that was for darn sure.

She shrugged one shoulder. "I'm just really busy."

"Yeah, I called you at the Institute but they said you were tied up." He eyed her pack as she stashed it into the trunk. "Finished for the day?"

Yes, but she wouldn't let him know that. "No. There's this report… "

As excuses went, that was lame. She couldn't think of a lie fast enough before he touched her. Just one hand on her arm and she wanted to melt. No! She straightened and leaned away from him.

He looked confused but soon smiled again. "Join me

for dinner? I'm just heading over to The Clubhouse now."

Dinner? Candlelight and wine and Rick, smiling and charming her out of her panties again? No way. Ariel and Max may have raised a flake but they hadn't raised a fool.

"I can't," she said. "I have this report to finish. I'm going to be up all night."

She flinched inwardly at her slip. That wasn't a good thing to say when all she wanted was to be up with him all night. Like last night. Nestled in his arms, hearing him finally open up about his family, the drive behind his ambition. But he must have missed her slip, because he just gave a quick nod.

"Okay," he said. "I won't bother you."

Whew. But then he kissed her. He tasted so good she wanted to keep kissing him forever. That treacherous thought brought her back to reality. Rick wasn't a forever kind of guy. He was all about right now, and she wasn't that kind of girl. She couldn't be. Her stupid heart was involved.

He ended the kiss too soon, darn her lack of control. He brushed his lips on her temple and straightened. "I'll talk to you tomorrow, then."

She couldn't watch him walk away without telling herself that soon he'd keep on walking. She hadn't really lost anything, right? Rick never made any promises. But she ached for what she'd thought they'd had. What she wished for, actually. A future together. A chance to make him realize that he was worth so much more than what Bill Chapman thought. Well, maybe she was a fool.

She waited until he entered The Clubhouse before driving back to her camp. It must have been the wind in her face that made her eyes tear.

She couldn't be crying over Rick.

***

Rick sat in the lounge of The Clubhouse, marking time until his take-out order was ready. He nursed his beer and peeled at the label's corner. He'd asked Harmony to join him for dinner, but she'd said she was busy. He blew out a breath. Busy? Since when did her work spill over into the evening? She'd seemed different there on the walk. Well, they had loved each other late into the night. Maybe she was just tired. He'd seen her tired before. He'd seen her angry. He'd seen her happy. But he'd never seen her so... Un-Harmony, maybe. There was no fire in those hazel eyes.

At least Bill and Tiffany were hell and gone from Cypress Corners. He could make the changes he'd decided on without the old man's interference. If he had to swallow one more comeback to his father's endless put-downs he'd burst. Tiffany hadn't hidden her continued interest, either. What a pair. He drank some more beer. But the project was on target, the money would come in on time, so Rick didn't have any worries there.

He thought for a moment. Maybe it was Harmony's work. God knew he could lose himself and his good mood if a job or contract didn't go just right.

He looked through the archway into the restaurant and rethought his conclusion. He spied Dr. Robbins sitting with a few people from the Institute, laughing and talking as they shared a meal. The Institute's director certainly didn't seem concerned about anything.

Rick put his bottle on the bar and stood, then made his way through the tables toward Dr. Robbins. He nodded greetings to the director's companions, a young man he'd seen around and the red-haired receptionist, and faced the doctor.

"Good evening, Dr. Robbins," he said.

"Rick, hello," Dr. Robbins said. He waved a hand at an empty chair at their table. "Join us?"

He shook his head. "No, thank you. I'm just picking up dinner. Have you spoken to Harmony?"

He ignored the speculative looks the other two exchanged, growing curious as Dr. Robbins' brow furrowed.

"Today? Why, yes. This afternoon we discussed her presentation on migration."

He knew nothing about that and didn't pretend to. "So she's still busy with it, I suppose."

Dr. Robbins blinked. "Not at all. We handed it over to the developers in a nice neat package this afternoon." He looked behind Rick and frowned. "Actually, I thought Harmony would be out with you tonight."

A server touched Rick on his elbow and he jerked. "Yeah?"

"Your order, Mr. Chapman," the skinny kid said. "It's on the bar."

"Thanks." He turned to Dr. Robbins. "That's my dinner. Have a good night."

He picked up his meal and headed to his house. A big juicy burger and a couple of beers later he sat on the couch, reliving the passion he'd shared with her on this spot. Where the hell was she tonight? Tucked into that cozy cabin of hers, poring over her notes. Too busy for dinner? Too busy for him, was more like it.   But what had he done?

It couldn't be that he kept his feelings from her. Aside from his admissions where Bill and his mother were concerned at least. She'd never asked for any pretty words, and never burdened him with any from her. He was the one who'd almost said he loved her. Thank God he hadn't made that mistake. Maybe those were just words, but they could do a lot of damage. That jerk Adam had probably promised her the friggin' moon when they were together.

He wasn't about to make promises he didn't intend to keep. All right. He wasn't a guy who ever made promises at all. They'd never talked about love or commitment. Hell, he'd never talked about what he was going to do next month let alone next year.

He had to keep his focus on what he wanted. Career. Proving himself. Chapman was everything. That had been his goal for years now. He closed his eyes. He wouldn't think about it. If Harmony said she was busy, she was busy. He'd never met anyone like her before, honest and upfront about everything. She wouldn't start playing games now.

He wouldn't play them with her, either. That was for damn sure. He'd take his cue from her and give her space. He wouldn't lose sight of his ultimate goal. Harmony's face filled his mind for an instant, her smile, her laugh. The sweet way she'd loved him last night.

Just for tonight he'd allow himself to think about something other than Chapman and the damn corporate ladder.

Tomorrow would come soon enough.

Chapter 16

After that awkward discussion outside the Institute Harmony hadn't seen much of Rick. It had been a full three weeks, actually. He'd probably been busy seeing the snack bar completed and she'd been tied up with her own work. It was none of his business if she chose to avoid him. It was getting harder and harder to think about him after what Tiffany had told her. But tonight was Christmas Eve. She didn't want to spend the night without him.

As if on cue, she heard the crunch of dirt and gravel beneath wide tires. Her heart skipped a beat in spite of her resolve as she stepped over to the door. She wore a thin red buttoned sweater over a pair of jeans, and nervously ran her hands over her sleeves before opening the door.

She'd strung little twinkling lights over the cabin and a few of the trees nearby, and the light seemed to dance over his hair, his face. He looked a touch apprehensive, nothing like the cock-sure guy he usually presented. He shifted the bottle of wine he carried from one hand to the other, a tentative smile on his lips.

She smiled in response. She didn't turned him away,

216

but for a second there she wished she had the willpower to do so.

"Merry Christmas," he said quickly. He held up a bottle of wine. "I thought we could share this."

She nodded and let him in. He glanced past her into the room, looking for what? she couldn't guess. He seemed relieved that the table was set for one.

He set the bottle down and looked around the cabin. "I'm kind of surprised you're here."

"Ariel and Max are up in Orlando for the week," she said. "Mom really makes a killing selling her organic pumpkin bread to the tourists. We'll get together tomorrow night."

He took off his jacket and draped it over a chair, rolling his shoulders as he did so. He almost seemed nervous. "I'm glad I stopped by, then."

She opened her mouth to tell she'd been all but wishing he'd come by, but finally nodded. "I am, too."

"Look, Harmony," he began. "I'm no good at this. I don't know what's been going on the past couple of weeks, but—"

"Don't you?" she cut in.

He blinked at her for a moment, then frowned. "Look, I'm not the one playing games here."

She laughed, but it wasn't a happy sound to her ears. "Games. You think I'm playing games."

He sat down and ran his fingers through his hair. "No, I... I don't know what I think. But look. It's Christmas. I wanted to spend it with you. No games."

She studied him for a moment. He seemed sincere, his gaze open. He looked good, wearing tan khakis and a cream fisherman sweater she wanted to rip right off him. Why not indulge herself this one last time? It was Christmas Eve. Maybe there'd be nothing in her stocking tomorrow. But she'd have Rick tonight. And if she lost a little bit more of her heart, who would it hurt besides herself?

"I want to spend tonight with you, too," she said.

He had the grace to look surprised even if he wasn't. He had to know that the minute she saw him there on her doorstep she'd wanted to jump his bones. It had been weeks since she'd been with him. More than her heart ached with the memory of their nights together. Her cheeks heated and she turned to the fridge.

"I hope you don't mind frozen turkey dinners," she said.

She'd bought two. Funny.

"Anything is fine," he said.

He opened the wine and she grabbed another glass from the cupboard. As she drank she set aside any lingering doubts about spending another night with him. Those fingers that curled around his wine glass, those eyes that sparkled at her. They ate their meals quickly. That was a relief, as she doubted she'd make it through dessert before throwing herself at him.

"The rec café is almost finished." He put their empty dinner trays next to the sink. "You have to come take a look."

Okay. Work. That helped her focus. She poured some coffee into a mug and handed it to him. "Why?"

He looked hurt, but that couldn't be right. "No reason, I guess. I just thought you'd be curious."

She was. Dying of it, really. She'd heard the construction that began early each morning, the whine of saws and the thrum of hammers faint from a couple of miles away. She knew from Dr. Robbins that the trails were all marked and in place. She just hadn't hiked them yet. She couldn't bring herself that close.

"I'm sure it's everything you promised the developers, Rick." She took her coffee and sat back down at the little table. "It'll make Chapman's investors happy, too."

"Yeah." He stared into his mug. "Happy."

He seemed young again, like the night they'd met Bill and Tiffany for dinner. Vulnerable. She wouldn't think of him that way, needing her comfort when he had his money, his career, and God knew how many women in Boston to keep him warm.

"What's next for you?" she asked, using the same words he'd given her before.

He shrugged and drank from his mug. "Back to Boston after the New Year."

She sipped her coffee, ignoring the sting as it burned her tongue. "Oh."

He put down his mug and grabbed her free hand. "I don't want to talk about Boston, Harmony. I don't want to talk about anything but you and me."

Her heart began to pound. "You and me?"

He brought her hand to his lips and kissed it. "Tonight, sweetheart. Together."

Oh. Tonight. Right. She willed her heart to slow and placed her mug on the table.

"That's what I want, too," she said. "Tonight."

Climbing into his lap, she wrapped her arms around his neck and kissed him.She stripped that sweater off him, taking a moment to breathe in his scent on the warm wool before letting it fall to the floor. His lips were urgent on her throat, her neck, as he pulled off her cardigan. He held her close against him, pressing against her center as she sighed his name.

"Ah, baby." The tip of his tongue played with the lace edge of her bra as he worked her jeans down her legs. "Harmony… "

He stood and tumbled her onto the bed and she put everything out her mind.   His motives might not have been clear when she'd first slept with him. Even that last time they slept together, when he'd shown her his vulnerability and a tiny piece of his heart.

Soon she thought of nothing but the feel of his hands on her skin. Her name on his lips as he kissed her everywhere.

Tonight she had no illusions. It was just sex, like it should have been from the beginning. Let her body have its way. Let her heart break again tomorrow.

Merry stinkin' Christmas.

***

"It's finished."

Rick waited for his father's response, holding the BlackBerry tight to his ear. His father said nothing for a long minute. Rick didn't say more. It was bad enough he needed Bill's approval. He'd be damned if he was going to beg for it.

"Good work, Chapman," Bill finally said. "I've been thinking. Since our visit I've realized you're worth something to Chapman Financial. More than I gave you credit for."

He held his breath. This was what he'd been waiting for. This was why he busted his ass down here in Florida for the last few weeks.

"And?" he asked.

"Come back to Boston, Rick. The top position is yours."

He closed his eyes and fisted his free hand at his side. He'd done it. At last.

"Thanks," he managed to say.

"See you in the office on Monday."

Bill broke the connection and Rick took a breath. Yes! Wait. Monday? That was only three days away. He had to talk to Harmony. She'd been different Christmas Eve, remote. But only at first. By the time they'd made it to her bed she'd been the warm, giving, passionate woman he'd known from the first.

"Boston," he said to himself. "Chapman. Everything."

He sank down into the leather couch. Yeah, everything. Money and prestige and all he'd strived for. But was it worth it? Could he leave what he had here with Harmony for what he knew awaited him in Boston? Which Harmony would he find when he told her about the promotion? The woman who kept herself too busy to see him and kept herself out of his bed? Or the one who begged him so sweetly to take her more than once the last time they were together?

"Damned if I know," he said. He came to his feet. "But I'm going to find out."

He found her at her camp, sitting at the end of the dock as the sunset danced over her. She hugged her knees to her chest, her back to him, and stared at nothing he could see. Or at everything, if he took in the big picture.

Trees dripping moss, birds flying low over the water, ripples on the lake from the breeze that kicked up. Cypress Corners might have been hot as hell in October but it was unbelievably comfortable by the end of the year.

Boston would be cold. Frozen and gray and heavy-skied above the soaring Chapman building. But it was home. Wasn't it?

"Harmony," he said.

She turned, just looked over her shoulder and gave him a small smile. She didn't seem surprised to see him. What did that smile mean? Happiness? Regret? Resignation? He wouldn't guess, not with his own emotions muddled.

"Hi, Rick."

She didn't get up as he walked toward her, his sneakers making no sound on the smooth planks of the dock. He'd miss her place, that was for sure. He sniffed the pines and the scent he would recognize as hers until the day he died.

"I have something to tell you." He settled beside her and mimicked her pose. "I'm going back to Boston."

She blinked and faced him, and a trick of the waning light made her eyes unreadable. "Oh? When?"

"I have to be at work on Monday."

She made a little sound in the back of her throat, like a hiccup, and nodded. "At Chapman. Working for your father."

He couldn't look at her. She knew how pitiful he was, then. Kowtowing to his father for any scrap of recognition. But the money and prestige… His mother's words still echoed in his mind. To prove himself a better man that Bill Chapman could ever be. This was all he knew. What he'd always wanted.

"Yeah," he said. "I'm the new Executive Officer in Charge of Foreign and Domestic Investments."

She didn't look terribly impressed at the title as she nodded again. "Congratulations. I know you've worked hard for this."

Her voice was flat, her body still. He needed some reaction from her. Something to show that she'd felt

225

something for him these past weeks.

"Tell me what you really think, Harmony," he said. "Don't sit there staring at me like I don't know you at all."

She blinked. "What?"

He stood and looked down at her. "Don't look at me like we haven't made love a hundred different ways until I know your body as well as my own."

She jumped to her feet and flung her hair out of her eyes. "Wait a minute."

Good. Now she looked angry, and he welcomed the change.

"Don't come here, telling me what to do, Rick," she said. "What do you want me to say? 'Oh, don't go?' 'Stay here with me forever?' Well, I'm not going to be the fool again."

He knew it. She thought he was like Adam, that jerk.

"You're not a fool," he ground out. "Just because one man broke your heart—"

"Adam didn't break my heart," she said. "And you won't either, believe me."

Chapter 17

Rick just stared at her. Harmony took a breath and held herself in check. She had to be strong. Not think about anything but letting him go. For him. For herself.

"Your work is important to you," she said. "I know that. I've always known that, from the day you stepped onto the ant pile. What I don't know is why you're putting all this on me."

He took a step closer and she braced herself.

"Damn it, Harmony." He raked his fingers through his hair. "I thought we had something here."

She shook her head. So did she. "You might be able to fool me, Rick. But don't fool yourself."

He grabbed her arms and she couldn't move. Not from the force of his grip but from the look in his eyes. If she didn't know better she'd think he really had feelings for her beyond the sexual.

"We're good together," he said.

She fought to keep her control. Her throat was tight, her heart racing.

He drew her closer. "I don't want to lose what we

have."

That did it. She had to break free now, or she would be his fool forever.

"What do we have, Rick?" she wrenched away from him and rubbed her arms where his fingers had been. She'd never be able to erase the memory of his touch. "Tell me what we have. Because I didn't see that it was anything but sex when it was convenient."

He cursed softly. "I know I haven't said the words, but—"

"Well, don't say them now," she warned, covering her ears. She brought her hands down slowly. "You've never lied to me. Don't start now."

She couldn't face him any longer, not with the hurt in his eyes and her heart in hers. Turning, she focused on a weed tangling around the dock platform beneath her.

She felt him step closer and steeled herself for whatever might come next.

"Come to Boston with me," he said.

Oh, God. She hadn't expected this. "No," she whispered.

He was silent behind her. She could hear him

breathing, could smell that Rick-scent that would always mark him as the last man to ever break her heart.

"That's it?" he asked. "Just, 'no?'"

What else could she say? Her parents needed her. They needed the money. To pay them back, she needed her job. She had to stay here. He had to go back.

There were no two ways about it, even if some lovesick jerk had temporarily taken over Rick's body. He'd be long gone before the plane touched down in Boston.

She faced him again, her arms crossed over her chest. "You need to go back, Rick. I don't. You need everything your father is offering."

She saw it in his face as his mouth thinned. She could almost hear the denial he wanted to make. But he couldn't deny it, not to her who knew just what Chapman Financial meant to him.

"You need the money and all it buys you," she went on. "Your new position, the recognition."

"But that doesn't... " His voice trailed off.

She wouldn't help him. Couldn't help him take a step he'd regret within a week.

"That doesn't what?" she asked. "Doesn't matter?"

She blinked rapidly to stop the tears before he could see them. "It's everything to you. And nothing to me."

"Harmony." His voice broke. "I can't change. I... I have to do this."

His eyes were a soft gray now, deep and sad. It would pass. He'd throw himself into his work and today would be a memory for him.

"I'm not asking you to change. We're different. You have your job there and I have my responsibilities here. End of story."

"Just like that?" He swallowed. "Just like that, you can let this go?"

She feigned an indifference she hadn't ever felt where he was concerned. "Why not? It was nice while it lasted, but I'm not going to lose any sleep over it."

He grabbed her again and for one long minute she let herself be held by the man she loved. His hands pressed against her spine, his heart beating against her cheek as she closed her eyes. But he wasn't really here. The man she loved didn't really exist at all.

"Tell me to stay, Harmony." He kissed her hair, her temple. "Tell me to stay and I will."

God, how she wanted to. But there was no place in Cypress Corners for him. She knew it if he didn't. He needed this job. He wanted this more than anything. She knew that. The tenderness in his eyes would soon fade if she made him give up his big chance.

"Go," she whispered. "Go and be happy."

He sucked in a breath and released her. "Fine. I'll go."

She watched him with a steady gaze as he stepped away from her. Then he turned away and she nearly cried out with relief. A few more steps and he was in the SUV. Another minute and he was driving away from her.

By Monday he'd be back in Boston, making deals and earning the money that would one day show Bill Chapman what he was worth. Maybe he'd think about her once in a while, when he was lonely or had a free night. But he'd never know what she felt. He'd never know he was worth so much more than money and deals to her. He was worth everything.

She crumpled onto the dock and sobbed until her throat was sore.

***

Rick threw his suitcase in the back of the SUV and slammed the door shut. How could he have misjudged a person so much? How had he so misconstrued what he and Harmony meant to each other? But he'd seen it. In her eyes when they'd filled with tears and in her body when she'd relaxed against him for that brief moment. But she wanted him out of her life? Fine! He'd go home and she could have the gators to keep her company.

When he'd left her camp he'd called the airlines. They'd had an open first-class seat on a flight to Boston tonight, so why the hell not? There was nothing here for him. She'd told him so.

She hadn't even come to see the snack bar. Not once. He'd changed more than the tile and the paint, but she didn't care. He'd taken what she'd taught him about nature to make changes that would be sound financially and environmentally. It didn't matter to her. Nothing he did mattered. He might as well go back to Boston. At least he had no illusions there. He knew nothing he did there mattered, either.

He took a long minute and looked up at the starry sky. It really was beautiful here, this place built with a mind to nature as well as money. Weird. But beautiful.

He drove to the Welcome Center and dropped the house key in the box where Tammy had told him to and drove out of the community. As he headed toward the airport he glanced in the rearview mirror. There was nothing there. His stomach clenched. He knew it was because of those special street lights, the ones that didn't throw any light upward. But to him it was more than that. It was as if Cypress Corners and everything that happened there had been just a dream, gone as quickly as he'd found it.

Well, that was what he'd wanted from the start, right? A diversion? No strings? He should be happy he got out of there before making a fool of himself for a woman he thought cared for him. He was happy. He slashed a thumb over his cheek and wiped it on his jeans. Damn it, he was happy.

By the time he arrived at his apartment, his head pounded. The meal on the plane had been less than filling. The three drinks he'd had hadn't helped. He dropped his bags on the marble-tiled foyer and walked through to the kitchen. Another beer, maybe. Hair of the dog and all that.

The message light on the phone blinked. A voicemail. It wouldn't be from her. She didn't have this number. No, it must be from Bill. While Rick was in the air his BlackBerry was turned off. His father must have called here as a last resort when he couldn't reach him at Cypress Corners or in the sky.

Well, this was what he wanted, right? Might as well jump right in.

"Hit the ground running, Rick," he told himself.

He punched the button and waited for his father's first edict.

"Chapman," his father's voice boomed. "Tammy at Cypress told me you left. Come to the house for dinner Sunday. I want to talk over some new acquisitions."

He cursed softly. He heard Tiffany's voice in the back, breathy and false as she added her own demands.

"Tiffany said to come at two. She said Jake might stop by."

With a click his "family" cut off. Maybe Jake would be there. Rick hadn't seen his brother in months. But Jake didn't like Tiffany any more than Rick did, and Bill could barely stand the second son who didn't do more than try

234

half-assed to work for the company.

"Maybe Jake has it right," he muttered.

He skipped the beer and stepped into the shower, letting the four steaming jets pound away his headache and his thoughts. With a fluffy towel from the heated towel bar wrapped around his waist, he padded into the bedroom and hit a button on the wall to turn on the state-of-the-art sound system. He collapsed on the satin comforter on his king-sized bed and stared up at the coffered ceiling.

This place was richly-appointed, a fact he paid plenty for every month. But when he closed his eyes he didn't picture the deep carpet, the magnificent view of the harbor or the gourmet kitchen he didn't use. No. He pictured a cozy one-room furnished with an old bed covered with a worn and unbelievably soft quilt. Nothing fancy, just warm and snug and occupied by the one person who could make any place feel like home. The only person since his mother who could ever make him feel like he belonged.

"Harmony."

He threw an arm over his eyes and fisted his hand. *Sleep, Rick. Forget.*

***

"We missed you Sunday."

Rick looked up from his desk and watched as Bill strode into the room. "Tiffany was upset."

He bit back the comment he wanted to make. "I was busy. I'm playing catch-up here."

His father adjusted the creases on his slacks and nodded at the simple explanation. Why wouldn't he agree? Wasn't work the most important thing? Why mess it up with family dinners.

"Jake couldn't make it, either," Bill said.

He opened his mouth to ask why but shook his head. Two sentences was about all Bill would spend on family discussions. Better to get on with business.

"I've been looking over the Aspen property," Rick said. "It's very promising."

Bill settled in the big leather chair facing Rick's desk. "Good. There's an investors' meeting Thursday morning. I want to have a few things to tempt them."

He nodded. Bill sat there at stared at him.

"What?" Rick asked him.

His father shrugged and stood. "Nothing. You look a little tired."

He waved a hand. "Like I said, Dad. I've been busy."

"Let me know what you have ready for Thursday's meeting."

With that Bill left the room. The exchange with his father was odd, but Rick wouldn't read it as fatherly concern. Not that he'd recognize it coming from Bill, even if it bit him in the ass.

He returned his attention to the papers on his desk. Acquisitions. Deals. Investments. Returns. This was what he'd trained for. Where he excelled. For once he'd take a page from his father's book and clear his mind of everything else.

By two o'clock the headache was back, beating dully behind his eyes. Pinching the bridge of his nose, he closed his eyes and pressed the intercom button on his phone.

"Yes, Mr. Chapman?" his new executive assistant said. She was young and shapely and no doubt hand-picked by Bill.

"Bring me a coffee and a couple of Advil, please," he said.

"Yes, sir."

The girl clicked off and he turned his chair toward the

view his new office provided, taking in the tall buildings and the crowded street thirty stories below. His headache pounded harder. Only looking up at the clouds he could see between two buildings brought him a bit of relief. Strange. He heard the door open behind him.

"Just leave it on the desk," he said. "And thanks."

"You're welcome," his brother said.

He spun his chair around and faced Jake. Younger than Rick by three years, Jake seemed even younger. Tanned and grinning, he looked like he just stepped off the cover of an adventure magazine. He wore an open flannel shirt over a thermal undershirt and rumpled khakis. Rick saw he still wore his black hair long to his shoulders and it was tied back in a ponytail. A gold hoop dangled from one ear. God, he was a sight for sore eyes.

"Jake."

"Hey, bro," Jake said.

He stood and crossed to him, wrapping him in a bear hug. "It's been a long time."

Jake hugged him back. "Yeah. Too long." He pounded Rick's back and they parted. "I thought I'd see what Bill's got you doing now."

He ignored the barb and sat back down. "I see you're still alive. In spite of yourself."

Jake slumped in the chair their father had just vacated and grinned. "Belize was a challenge, but I'm still alive and kickin'." He lost his smile. "Which is more than I can say for you."

He waved a hand. "I'm just trying to acclimate myself to the new position, Jake."

Jake blew out a breath. "Yeah. Executive Officer of big money, and ruler of all finances in the free world. You wanna tell me what happened in Florida?"

He winced and took the two Advil with a gulp of coffee. "I don't know what you're talking about."

"Yeah," Jake said again. "I got an earful from dear Stepmom, along with a couple of gropes. She said something about some tree-hugger?"

He kept his face immobile, saying nothing.

"Come on, bro," Jake said softly. "Spill."

He looked into his brother's eyes. Dark like their mother's, they were clear and sharp and concerned. What the hell? He spilled.

Chapter 18

Jake let out a whistle and ran his fingers through his hair, freeing a few strands from his ponytail. "So what are you going to do?"

Rick's throat was tight, but he was just thirsty, right? He drained the rest of his now-cold coffee. "Nothing. I'm going to do nothing. She told me to leave and I did."

"Just like that?"

He looked at his brother. Jake lounged in the chair. He appeared relaxed but his eyes showed his full attention from beneath lowered lids. Damn.

"Look, Jake." He spread his hands in front of him. "Harmony made her choice. It wasn't me."

"What did you choose? Tell me that one."

He stood and paced behind his desk. "I chose Chapman, damn it. It's what I've wanted forever. Since Mom died." He met Jake's gaze. "This is what I chose."

"Man." Jake shook his head. "You sound just like Bill."

He fisted his hands. "Don't give me that bullshit! You're not the one working his ass off for this company, here every friggin' day no matter what."

"Hey, I'm only telling you what I see. You give yourself to this place and you lose, bro."

"This is my career, damn it! I don't know anything else. I vowed to win and this is my reward."

"You're losing it, Rick. Stay here and you'll turn into our father."

"That's not fair," he growled. "You play at Chapman. You scale mountains and jump off bridges and when you're bored you come back here to make a little money. I can't do that."

"Why not? You don't owe Bill anything."

He felt his anger leave in a rush as he covered his face with his hands. "I don't do this for Bill."

The silence stretched for several minutes. He heard Jake shift in the chair and lifted his head to find his brother leaning toward him. Jake's eyes looked wet.

"She's gone, Rick," Jake said softly. "She's been gone a long time."

He knew this in his head. But in his heart? It was like she just died.

"It's not just my promise. This is what I'm made for.

This is what I want."

"Then why do you look like shit?"

He smirked at him. "Thanks."

"Now tell me what you really want," Jake said.

What did he want? He wanted passion and comfort. Strength and sweetness. He wanted to feel like he did when he was with…

"God, Jake." He swallowed hard. "I want her. I want Harmony."

"Then go for it."

He rubbed his brow and winced again. "It's not that easy."

Jake stood and walked around the desk. "Seems easy to me." He put his hand on Rick's shoulder. "And it seems like you should fly back down there and make her see that, too."

"No." He sat back in his chair. "She told me to leave and I left. End of story."

Jake shook his head but didn't press him again. He didn't know if he was grateful for that or a little pissed off.

"I talked to Cassie last week," Jake said.

Cassie. Their wild little sister who was off in Europe.

"Man," Rick said. "Do I want to know what she's up to?"

"She got kicked out of another school."

He snorted. "Big surprise. I doubt she's ever going to graduate."

"She runs around with those Euro-trash friends of hers. They don't care if they finish their degrees or not."

"I wish she'd just finish and come home." He fiddled with the pens on his desk. "I haven't been able to reach her for months."

Jake chuckled. "I think the kid turns off her phone. Wouldn't you?" He walked toward the door. "Let's get together for dinner."

He thought of his schedule for the coming week. What the hell? "Thursday night?"

Jake nodded. "Don't work too hard," he said as he left.

He laughed at Jake's parting shot. He thought about his siblings then, each screwed up in their own way because of Bill. He wasn't kidding with Jake. He didn't want to know what trouble Cassie was getting into. Maybe Bill's attention would come in time to help one of them.

Before Jake killed himself or Cassie got into a mess Bill's money couldn't buy her out of.

He thought about all Bill had finally bestowed on him at Chapman. He had his father's attention now. Finally.

It would have to be enough.

***

Harmony woke up, her head pounding. She turned and nearly threw up over the side of the bed.

"Shouldn't have eaten at The Clubhouse last night," she grumbled. "Darn rich food."

She sat on the edge of the bed and braced herself with her arms while the room settled. Rubbing her temples, she took slow even breaths. True, she hadn't been sleeping well since Rick left two weeks ago. It seemed she saw him around every stinkin' corner of the property. Dr. Robbins only asked about him once, thank goodness. She hated lying, especially to him. But it was better if everyone thought she and Rick hadn't been lovers while he was here. Because if they knew he'd used her, taken advantage just to further Chapman's concerns, what did that make her?

It was bad enough Hettie knew. But as eccentric as she seemed, Harmony knew she could count on the woman to keep her secrets. Yes, she knew they'd slept together. What she didn't know was how hard Harmony had fallen for him.

She washed her face and felt better right away. That was weird. As she brushed her hair, she focused her mind on the meeting with the developers at the end of the week. Since Rick left, she'd found that they welcomed her input. So she accompanied Dr. Robbins to the meetings and also discovered that she liked presenting her own work to a table surrounded by people with more money than she'd ever see. But they treated her well. They respected her. Darn it, it felt good.

Another day at the Institute, another day to avoid Rick's phone calls. Becky didn't even page her any more. She just took a message and left a little pink note on Harmony's desk in the lab. It was a nice stack of pink notes by now, but she couldn't bear to throw them away. So there they still sat, pink, perky and expectant.

She finished getting dressed and rode into the village. Several people she recognized called out greetings to her as she wove her way through the Village Center toward the Institute, and she waved back. Residents and people who worked at the Welcome Center called her name as she rode past. Strange, but it felt good. Maybe she should think about moving into the village. Hettie had been pressing her to do just that for weeks now. Construction on the recreation center would start in a few months. Why put off the inevitable?

Just a couple of months ago the thought would've seemed ridiculous. Frightening. Maybe she'd go into the Welcome Center and see what they had available. She snorted. Maybe Rick's house was still vacant. No way. She couldn't bear to be in the place he'd so recently occupied. It was bad enough she saw him around every corner.

Her scooter wobbled beneath her and she touched her left foot down to steady herself as she turned a corner. No. She couldn't drive past that house without thinking of what they'd done inside. What she'd done. She'd been wild and free and had taken full advantage of the willing man beneath her. Rick had been in as big a hurry, his body ready for her in an instant. Her body flushed with the memory. Why, they hadn't even had time to put on a condom.

The truth hit her right in the belly. She skidded to a stop and covered her mouth with her hand.

"Oh, God."

She counted in her head and knew. In a flash she just knew. She was pregnant! In her mind she saw a flash of something, a smiling baby with thick dark hair and bright eyes. Rick's son or daughter. Oh, God.

She got off her scooter and walked it the block or so to the Institute. She didn't trust herself to ride there safely, the way her hands were shaking. Heck, her whole body was shaking.

"Hey, Harmony!" Becky called.

She turned and waved to the girl sitting on a bench beneath a large crepe myrtle tree. She parked the scooter and took off her helmet. Her cheeks burned. That was silly. No one knew about Rick or the baby. If there was a baby. Well, she wasn't going to wait to find out.

She walked over to Becky on shaky legs. The girl was drinking a yogurt smoothie and just the thought of drinking the thick rich shake, sweet and creamy and a little sour, made her stomach twist again.

"Hi, Becky." She took a breath as the nausea passed, leaving her heart racing. "When you go back in could you tell Dr. Robbins I'm here but I'll be a little late?"

"Sure."

Becky's brow furrowed and she put down the smoothie. Harmony watched the shake ease its way back down the straw and gulped.

"Harmony?"

She looked at Becky again and shook her head. "What?"

"Are you all right?" Becky smiled a little. "Sorry, but you looked a little pale there for a minute."

She swallowed as she tried to slow her racing pulse. "I'm fine." She gave the girl what she hoped was a smile. "Really, Becky. I'm fine."

Becky opened her mouth but Harmony didn't give her a chance to ask her anything else. She waved and turned away, heading for the storefronts across the street. If her suspicions were right, in a couple of months no one would have any question about it.

She hurried toward the shop on the corner, an old-fashioned drugstore and soda fountain that carried everything from penny candy to the newest pregnancy tests. She hurried past the glass and chrome canisters filled with red-hots and other treats, the sweet smell almost sickening her again. Well, she sure wasn't shopping for taffy. Huh-uh. The sooner she knew, the better. She turned down an aisle of the store to a section she'd never visited before.

Less than fifteen minutes later, in the privacy of the ladies' room at the Institute, her answer was a double line where there should have been one. She crouched down on the floor of the bathroom and leaned her head against the cool tiles behind her. A baby. What would Rick say?

She stood and dropped the test stick into the garbage can. "He's not going to find out," she said as she washed her hands. She couldn't tell him. It was a moot point anyway. He wouldn't want the child. He'd probably think it was nothing more than an inconvenience.

Wiping her hands, she stared in the mirror as another thought struck her. It could be worse. What if Rick wanted to help her raise it? A sense of protectiveness flared in her and she held a hand over her belly.

"It's never going to happen," she said, only half to herself.

He'd fly in now and then to see them, throw money at them like Bill had done. Then he'd go back to his work.

There would always be his work. She wouldn't let Rick's driving ambition turn their child into a carbon-copy of himself.

An abandoned child desperate for its father's attention.

Chapter 19

Harmony waited for the morning sickness to pass, nibbling on one of the rice cakes she kept handy beside her bed. She stared up at the draped ceiling. Just a few more minutes and a spoonful of apple vinegar and she'd be fine. Good thing she'd listened to her mother when she handed folks advice for everything from arthritis to insomnia to morning sickness. Ariel Brooks certainly knew her stuff.

She should really talk to her mother. Nearly a week had passed since she'd learned she was pregnant, and keeping the news to herself was driving her crazy. She didn't want anyone at the Institute to know about it yet. She'd kept any exchanges with Hettie to a minimum, too. God knew she couldn't tell Rick. But she was happy about the baby, this little bit of her and Rick. She smiled and sat up slowly. She'd make sure he or she was loved, and what better start was there than Max and Ariel Brooks showering the child with affection and good thoughts?

"Maybe Ariel will have a reading of the baby's past lives," she laughed to herself.

As she'd gotten used to, the nausea passed quickly

and she dressed. Her parents were due for a visit. Maybe she should wade through that growing pink pile of messages at the Institute and see if there was one from them. She threw on a sweater and hopped on her scooter. As she made her way from the camp, the cool air invigorating on her cheeks, she still thought about those phone messages. She'd glimpsed Rick's name on one slip yesterday, and her fingers had itched to pick it up. But, as the more recent ones in the stack showed, it just had his name and telephone number. No message, no endearment. What did she expect? A stinkin' Valentine?

Something niggled at her, something that made her stop at a point where the path grew rockier and more overgrown. Precisely where over the past three weeks she'd purposely kept her gaze fixed forward. He'd asked her to come and look at the rec café before he left, and more than once. She'd resisted. Why take an interest in his work? He was interested enough for the both of them But now she felt like she had to see it. It was the reason they'd gotten together in the first place. It had meant so darn much to him while he was here.

"What the heck?" She stepped on the pedal and

turned the scooter in the direction of the café. Built on the site where she'd first seen him.

"Be strong, Harmony." Don't be a fool, she mentally added.

As she got closer, the path became smoother and she could make out the recreation area up ahead. But something wasn't right. The nature trails were well marked but their edges were soft enough to look as if they'd developed over years instead of weeks. She could see hikers and children making use of the paths, some hurrying and some taking their time. At the center of the activity was a building, nestled under a canopy of trees.

She stopped the scooter and stared. "Wow," she breathed.

The rec café was nothing like she'd envisioned. It was made of stone and framed with rough-hewn wood planks, and the paint that colored the stucco walls was a green as soft as the underside of a scrub buckwheat leaf. People bustled in and out of the double doors, talking and smiling as they carried their little brown bags of treats and cups of coffee to the round iron tables set on the small stone patio. She drove closer and parked the scooter in the bike rack set off to one side of the building.

She saw bottles of juices and nectar on the tables and in people's hands and could smell cinnamon and vanilla. Suddenly her mouth watered. She smiled. So much for morning sickness. This baby wanted to eat and it wanted to now. She stepped off the scooter and walked into the little retreat.

There was a line from the counter to the door, and she stepped aside to allow a happy patron to make their exit.

"Harmony!"

She turned at the familiar voice and stared at her mother, who bustled behind the counter. "Mom?"

Ariel smiled at her as she finished a transaction at the cash register. "And five is twenty." She waved over a young woman working behind the counter to take up her position and wiped her hands on her tie-dyed apron. "Hello, dear."

"Mom, what are you doing here?"

Her mother grinned and jabbed her thumb toward the man deftly working the cappuccino machine. "I couldn't let him work by himself, could I?"

She blinked in the man's direction. "Dad?"

Max winked at her. "Hi, hon," he called over the hissing and gurgling of the machine.

She took a step back and settled on a stool near the counter. "What the… ? Mom, why are you guys working here?"

Ariel pointed to the large bake case dominating one wall of the rec café. Glass plates topped with white doilies sat on the racks inside, holding snacks Harmony could identify in a heartbeat.

"Tofu cheesecake, Mom?" She smiled. "Carob fudge brownies and cinnamon apple tartlets?"

"That's right," Ariel said. "I supply all the treats for the joint. Your Dad makes the coffee."

"How did you… ?" She was floored. "How?"

Ariel took her hand and sat beside her. "Rick."

She was grateful for the seat beneath her bottom as she tried to clear her head. Rick? She must have heard wrong. "Rick? I know he was involved in the staffing, but… "

"He changed the design, too," Ariel said. "To make it fit in better, he told us. To put it in balance. He arranged for your father and me to supply the place." She winked.

"Working here was your father's idea. But what the heck? Maybe we could settle down a few months out of the year. It beats trucking up to Orlando every weekend."

Her head was spinning, and it had nothing to do with the tiny being nestled inside her. Her mother's explanation made no sense. Yet it filled her with a cautious spark of hope.

If Rick could change his mind about the café, maybe he could change his attitude too. Maybe he didn't think Cypress Corners was so messed up after all, not if he could see the merits of blending development with nature.

"Maybe I was wrong," she said to herself.

"About what, dear?" Ariel asked. "When I spoke to Rick last—"

"You… " She faced her mother. "You spoke to him?"

"Yes, dear. Before he went back to Boston."

She looked around at the successful and lovely little café. "Before. Then he knew about… He must have made these changes weeks ago."

"And called your father and me," Ariel added. "I think we're a pretty good fit, don't you?"

Her dad was humming as he bopped around behind the counter. Her mother, with her unruly hair tied in a neat ponytail with a scarf that matched her apron. Harmony had to admit her parents looked too cute and capable in the place. This place that Rick had changed to suit its environment instead of intruding upon it. Could it be he really understood it now? The way everything should be in balance?

"Mom." She took both her mother's hands in hers. "I have to tell you something. I... I need your opinion."

"Mine?" Ariel started to stand. "Let me get my crystals, and—"

"No. We don't need the crystals."

Her mother settled back on the stool, her brow furrowed. "What is it, dear?"

"Rick's stepmother told me something when she was here. Something horrible. I didn't want to believe it."

"What did she say?"

She took a breath. "She said that Rick used me to further his career."

There. It was out. To her great relief her mother was smiling. Relief and surprise. That wasn't right.

"That's ridiculous, Harmony," her mother said. "Rick didn't use you. He cares for you a great deal."

She blew out a breath. "I wish I could believe that."

Her mother started to say something more, but held back. "I can't tell you what's in Rick's heart, dear. But I can see yours. You love him."

Yes, she loved him. Him and the baby she carried, but she couldn't say that. Not yet.

"Yes, I love him."

"Does he know?"

"God, no." Harmony stood and crossed to the cooler near the counter and grabbed a bottle of peach nectar. "Put this on my account, Dad."

Max chuckled and made a check in the air with one finger. "I'm starting a tab, hon."

She returned to her mother and sat again. "I didn't tell him I love him." She opened the bottle, drank down the sweet cool nectar and licked her lips. "What good would it have done?"

Ariel shrugged. "That's between the two of you. But that's not all I wanted to tell you."

"Oh, brother. What next?"

"We know about the back account, dear."

She couldn't protest, so she just nodded mutely. "And?"

"There's no need, Harmony." Her mother shrugged and placed a hand on her hip. "Your father and I are doing just fine, especially with a direct market for these goodies."

"But I have to pay you back, Mom." Her eyes began to tear. "What Adam did... What I let him do to both of you was horrible."

"We never blamed you," Ariel said. "Not once. Adam was no good."

"He was a bastard," she muttered.

"Yes, he was," her mother said. "But boy, was he great at hiding it. I couldn't even read his aura, he had such a wall of charm put up."

Charm. Yeah. Adam had charm in spades.

"But still, Mom. All your savings... It still stings that he used your hopes that way."

"We were foolish. But he only took our money. He took your heart." Ariel tilted her head to one side. "Or did he? I think someone else has it now."

"Yes." She capped her bottle and set it on the counter.

"Fat lot of good it does me. We all know how great my judgment is where men are involved."

"Don't do it, sweetheart." Her mother shook her head, the tiny bells hanging from her ears softly tinkling. "Don't let Adam ruin what you could have with Rick."

"And what's that? A life in Boston? I don't think so. He might have made these changes here, but could he settle here? Be happy here? With me?"

"I don't know. But don't let your past judgment cloud your mind now. I've seen Rick's aura, remember?"

She shrugged. "So you said."

Ariel didn't appear to take offense. She just smiled again. "His aura is pure, Harmony. Yes it's cloudy, even when I saw him a few weeks ago. But he has a good soul."

Her mother stood and patted her arm. "Finish your juice. You could use it."

She started but her mother just smiled again and stepped behind the counter. She couldn't know about the baby. Could she?

She finished the bottle and capped it once more, fiddling with the label wrapping the wide neck. Rick's aura was pure, huh? She snorted. What did that mean?

Her hand settled on her belly and she felt that spark of hope flare inside her. Rick had made these changes. He'd found a way to let her parents take care of themselves, something she'd never even considered. To see them with such purpose, the obvious enjoyment they felt working for themselves, told her she'd approached the aftermath of Adam's scheme in the wrong way. She'd thought money was the only thing Adam had taken from them. Who would have thought that Rick would see more where she hadn't?

Had she been wrong, letting him go back to Boston? Was there was a place for him at Cypress Corners? Her heart lifted a fraction. Was there a place for him with her?

"Maybe," she whispered to herself. "Maybe."

She smiled and tapped the counter. "How about a slice of cheesecake, Mom?"

Chapter 20

"Yeah, thanks." Rick tapped the pen in his hand on the arm of his leather desk chair as he stared out at the gray sky outside his office, waiting for the same answer he'd gotten for weeks now. This afternoon was no different. "Just tell her… Just tell her I called."

The line went dead and he let out a breath. He turned in his chair and dropped the phone back in the cradle. Why wouldn't she call him back? It was almost a month since that horrible day out on her dock and she hadn't tried to reach him. Not once. If he had any pride left, he'd stop calling her. But just the thought of the receptionist saying his name to Harmony made him feel a little better. She'd have to think about him then, at least for a second. She'd have to acknowledge… something.

He should just focus on his job. God knew it took up his time during the day and his mind during the night. Aside from a stolen afternoon here and there at the health club, his life was all lonely dinners and working until after midnight. But he only had his work. The biggest deal of his career which would prove he was the man for this job.

Chapman was gearing up for a big push, bringing on investors to pour their money into the sprawling development planned for the Aspen property. Aspen. The thought was tempting. He needed a change of scenery. It was unusual for him, but he hadn't been anywhere since taking this job. Not to a bar or a restaurant since the dinner with Jake, except to coddle some Chapman investors. Maybe he'd fly out to Aspen. Do a little skiing. Do a little drinking. What the hell, right?

Looking out the window he saw the streets below were layered with old snow, brown and sooty even from up here. The city was cold and damp and lonely. His office was climate-controlled, of course. Comfortable enough that he'd shed his jacket and worked in his shirtsleeves. Yet he wasn't really comfortable, not in his office and not in the city. This was nothing like what home should feel like. He'd never thought about Boston that way before, but he did now.

Jake had taken off for parts unknown a couple of days earlier, and Rick felt his loss keenly. At least he'd talked to his sister for a few minutes last week. The kid sounded okay, if overly cheerful. Something was up, but he didn't have the strength to worry about it. Besides, who was he to give her advice?

He'd dodged a few more dinner invitations to Chez Chapman. That was a relief. Bill at home was something he'd been spared since he'd left Rick's mother. He certainly saw his father enough at work. He wouldn't extend his sucking-up to after hours. Or to Tiffany.

He tried to focus on the file in front of him. What was up with this deal again? Man. Oh, yeah. Where to put the second martini bar. Huge chunks of ice—purportedly carved from the mountains, but that was a crock—through which the different mixtures would trickle down into the waiting customer's frosty glass. Very trendy. He didn't even care. He shut the folder.

This was what he'd wanted. Even his talk with Jake hadn't changed that. He admitted he wanted Harmony, too. Well, he was done groveling. She didn't want to call him back? Fine.

"Screw it," he muttered.

"Sounds like an invitation."

He looked up to find Tiffany in his doorway. She was dressed in her usual attire, short skirt and tight blouse. He could smell her overpowering perfume from where he sat. Something French, probably. Expensive. Her practiced smile put him as much on edge as her scent.

"I'm busy," he said.

"Your secretary wasn't at her desk." She shrugged and shut the door. "Silly girl. If I worked under you, I'd be… eager to please."

He let that one go, as obvious as it was. "Like I said. I'm busy."

She walked to his desk and propped a hip against the edge. Reaching closer, she fingered the folder in front of him. "Work. You and your father. You're cut from the same cloth."

Hardly. "Get out, Tiffany."

She slid closer, her leg brushing his arm. The rasp of her pantyhose sliding over his shirt sleeve scratched against his brain and he pulled away.

"What do you want?" he asked.

"Been awhile, Rick?" She reached out and brushed the hair off his forehead. When he jerked his head back at the contact she laughed. "You're very jumpy."

That was it. He stood. "Leave me the hell alone,

Tiffany. It wasn't cute the first time and it's not cute now."

She pouted her lips. "What are you talking about? I'm just making conversation."

"You're my father's wife, damn it."
She reached for him again and he cursed.

"That's a pity, since you want me," she said. "It's obvious."

"The only thing that's obvious is how pitiful you are."

"Tell me you don't want me." Her eyes narrowed and she pointed a long-nailed finger in his face. "Tell me you haven't always wanted me."

He would have laughed if he was watching this on television. Who said lines like that outside of a soap opera? But here? Now? This was just sad.

"Are you kidding me?" he countered. "Why the hell would I want you?"

Her botox-ed forehead didn't pucker as she raised her eyebrows. "It's that girl, isn't it?"

"Who?"

"Melody."

"Harmony."

"Whatever. You're still horny for her? I don't believe

it."

"Get out," he said again. "I'm not talking about her. Not with you, of all people."

She closed the short distance between them and smiled, the expression hideous at such close range. "Why not? She seemed to have no problem talking to me about you."

He scoffed. "Right. You barely spared her two words at dinner that night."

"True." She moved away from him at last and ran her fingers over the desk. "But I went to her camp."

"You did what? When?" He shook his head. "Never mind that. Why?"

"I wanted to see how the little tree-hugger lived. I saw her little tent or whatever. The lake, the trees. It was pretty enough. I liked the outside shower." Her mouth turned down at the corners. "Did you screw her there?"

He fisted his hands at his sides to keep from wrapping them around her neck. "What did you say to Harmony, Tiffany?"

"I told her what Bill said, Rick. That he told you to seduce her to get her on Chapman's side."

"Son-of-a… Are you out of your mind?"

"It's true."

"Goddamn it!" He stalked over to her and grabbed her arms. "Bill never told me any such thing. If he had—"

"If he had you would have done it," she snapped. "He says 'jump' and you ask 'how high?'"

He pushed her away from him. "Shut up. I can't believe you told her that. You lying bitch."

She ran her hands over the sleeves of her blouse, adjusting the shoulders so the neckline fell to a deep V once more. "Call me what you want. I'm honest enough to admit what I am."

"A money-grubbing slut?"

"At least I know what I want and I go after it." She walked to the door. "You're too busy kissing up to Daddy to go after what you want."

"And that's you, I suppose? Not in a million years."

She ran her eyes over him and curled her lip. "You don't have the balls to go after what you want, Rick. Maybe you're not like your father after all."

In a flash he felt his chest open up and his head clear as her words made their unintentional mark. "You're goddamned right. I'm not like him. Now I'm tired of saying it, 'Mom.' Get the hell out."

She smirked again and left, passing his secretary as she stepped into the doorway. "Get out of my way."

The girl frowned in confusion and looked at Rick. "Mrs. Chapman had me go down to the copy room but they didn't have anything for you. Did you need something?"

So she'd gotten the girl out of the way so she could what? Seduce him? The conniving little…

"No, thanks," he said. She turned to leave and he called out to her. "Wait. Tell my father I need to see him. Right away."

She nodded and hurried out of his office, closing the door behind her. Rick sat back down and went over what Tiffany had said. Oh, not the innuendo and out-and-out propositions. What she divulged about going to see Harmony. It made sense now. Ever since Bill and Tiffany's visit she'd been different. He thought about Christmas Eve. Most of the night she'd been cool and reserved. But if she believed anything that Tiffany said, and Rick was sure it was more than the bitch admitted today, it was little wonder she hadn't wanted to come with him. Or to ask him to stay.

She thought he'd used her? For his friggin' career? No. Even in the beginning, when he took her to dinner to get her on his side, he'd wanted her. For her, nothing more. What man would want anything more?

"Not me."

"'Not you?'" Bill walked in and shut the door. "What are you muttering about?"

Rick faced his father, the man whose good opinion he'd sought for so long. For too damn long. He stood up. "This job, Dad. It's not me."

"What the hell are you talking about? I groomed you. Taught you everything you know. You're made for this job."

"I don't want it."

Bill stared at him, his mouth open. Then he scowled. "I thought you had your priorities straight, Chapman. I thought you'd proven yourself to me. I thought you wanted the damn job."

"I did. Before." Man, it felt great to say the words. He took a second or two to say them in his head again. "But I don't want it now."

His father blinked a few times. "But... It's what

you've always wanted. What I wanted for you."

"Since when? I've wanted your approval all this time, and now—"

"You have it." His father stepped closer. "You have it all, Rick."

Confusion and something else showed on his father's face. Desperation? He doubted it. He put on his jacket and smoothed down his tie.

"Tell me what you want, Rick. More money? Why the hell not? The Aspen project is due to bring in a ton of it."

Rick walked over to the rack in the corner grabbed his coat. He shrugged it on. "I hope the money keeps you warm, Dad." He grabbed his laptop and briefcase and shoved them under his arm. "Me? I'm through. Through living up to a promise I never should have made. Through kissing up to a man who couldn't give a crap about me until I added enough to the bottom line."

"You can't quit, Rick." His father's voice stopped him. It almost sounded… warm. Real. Like the man cared. "I need you here."

Rick shook his head. "Well, I don't need this. It's too

little, too late. I don't need you or your approval anymore."
He walked past his father and into the hall. "Let Jake take
over the position. If you can convince him, that is. Good
luck with that."

He didn't clearly hear what his father said after that,
the mutterings, the curses. He was through with all of it and
every word he'd said was true. He didn't need Bill
Chapman or his money. He didn't need this job or the
prestige it brought.

The elevator ride to the lobby was long and gave him
time to recall every beautiful word he'd said. God, it felt
great. He felt great. No more headache, no more chest
constriction. He was almost high with relief.

Stepping outside onto the crowded sidewalk, he
sucked in a breath. The air was cold but it felt wonderful as
it bit into his lungs. No, he didn't need Chapman Financial.
He only needed one thing.

Harmony.

Chapter 21

The airport was crowded with families eager to leave the chill of New England for the fun and sun in Florida. Rick was leaving the chill, all right. For good.

His cell beeped and he checked the screen. Jake. Thank God.

He answered with a smile. "Yeah, Jake."

There was a moment of silence before Jake chuckled in his ear. "Bro, you even sound better."

He smiled into the phone. "Bill told you?"

"Yep." Jake whistled. "And was he pissed! He just doesn't get it."

"He never did." He checked his watch. "I can't talk long. My flight's boarding in ten minutes."

"I just wanted to wish you a safe trip. When will you be back?"

"To Boston? Not anytime soon. Come down to Cypress."

He could almost see him shaking his head. "Gotta get to Aspen."

"God, no." Rick sat up. "You're working for Chapman?"

"A little." Jake laughed again. "Let's say the place is gonna have a climbing wall the likes of which they'd never seen before."

"Now, that I can believe." He was quiet then, just existing in the same space for the moment. "Keep in touch, okay?"

"Yeah, bro. You too."

He slipped the cell back into his pocket. Let Bill just try to mold Jake into his corporate image. No friggin' way.

The plane ride seemed to take forever. Waiting in the car rental line was no picnic, either. The place was packed with families eager to start their holiday, shuffling bags and kids as they inched toward the counter.

He had to come to his senses now, in the middle of school vacation season? At least he wasn't getting a minivan. That line was around the block.

He refrained from tapping his foot as he stood behind a large woman with a toddler perched on her hip. Another child, a girl about four years old, held tightly to the woman's other hand.

"We need a car seat," the woman called to the guy in front of her.

The guy, the husband and head of the brood, nodded and waved a map over his shoulder. "Yeah, Marie. I know."

"Are we going to see Mickey today?" the little girl asked the woman. She wore her favorite mouse on her shirt and clutched one in her arms. When neither parent answered right away, she turned to Rick. "Are we?"

He stared down at her, at her hopeful face and big blue eyes. "I don't know, sweetheart. But I bet you'll see him soon."

She nodded, her black curls bouncing. "He lives down here, you know," she said. "Dreams come true here, too."

He laughed lightly. "They do?"

"Yep. 'When you wish upon a star.'" She nodded sagely. "The song says so."

"Come on, Haley," the woman said. She grabbed the girl's hand and gently dragged her toward another waiting area. "Daddy's getting our luggage into the car and then we're off!"

The little girl waved at Rick. "Bye! I'm going to see Mickey. I hope your dreams come true!"

He watched her family, the dad harried and the mom put-upon but both showing the same spark of excitement that their daughter did. Wishing upon a star... He'd never done that. He thought about the gorgeous starry sky above Cypress Corners and knew what wish he'd make if he got the chance.

Dreams came true here, huh? He hoped so.

***

Harmony settled cross-legged on her dock, looking out over the cool water. It was the middle of February and the sun warmed her through her sweater. A soft breeze teased her hair as she closed her eyes and leaned her head back. The nausea of the morning long passed, she opened her eyes and breathed in deeply. She stared at the pines and bare branches of the oaks and maples surrounding her lake. This was a beautiful place. Now that she'd seen for herself that development here wouldn't necessarily be ugly or intrusive, she looked forward to bringing her child to the recreation area that would be set here.

There would be a playground equipment. A launch

for canoes and paddleboats. Another snack bar or maybe a hotdog stand. She could deal with that. The people, too. Dr. Robbins. Sweet, scandalous Hettie.

She hadn't formed any other lasting friendships yet, but she liked joining the others from the Institute at The Clubhouse for dinner now and then. Even Tammy at the Welcome Center was nice once Harmony got to know her better. She hadn't always felt at ease on property, away from her camp. Now she felt like Cypress Corners itself was her home. It was a nice feeling.

But something was missing. Someone was missing. Rick. She glanced down at her belly, at the swelling just beginning to show. He deserved to know. Oh, not all of it. She wouldn't tell him she loved him. But he deserved a chance to try to be a father to their baby. Their baby deserved the shot Rick never got.

She'd call him. She'd head toward the village and use the pretty little silver cell phone Dr. Robbins had given her. It was only good for telling the time out here at her camp, but she knew right where it picked up a signal, where it gave a friendly little chirp she'd ignored up until now.

Determined, she stood and brushed her hands over the

front of her jeans and walked down the dock. She heard the crunch of tires on gravel and looked toward her cabin.

A little red car—a Jeep, she could make out from here—parked in front of her cabin but she couldn't see the driver from this angle. Curious, she stepped around a fat cypress trunk and looked again. There was no one in the Jeep so she walked up to her cabin and pulled open the door. And froze.

Rick sat on the bed, his hands folded between his knees. Her heart tripped and she nearly did on the thick rag rug. She had to be hallucinating. She'd just been thinking about him!

"Rick?"

He glanced up at her. Wearing jeans and that fisherman sweater again, he looked incredible. His hair was mussed and his clothes rumpled but the small smile on his lips made her insides quiver.

"Hey, Harmony."

She let the door softly bang shut behind her. "I was just going to call you."

When he looked skeptical she held up her little phone, dangling it by its wrist cord.

"You get a signal out here?" he asked.

"No. I was going to—" She shook her head. "What are you doing here?"

He shrugged one of those broad shoulders and stood. "Where else would I be?"

No. She wouldn't dare believe it. She slipped the phone into her pocket. "Where? How about Boston?"

He laughed, a deep sound she realized she'd missed as much as his kisses.

"Boston isn't home for me anymore, sweetheart," he said. "Home is here."

She took a step back and leaned against the wood-framed wall. "W-what?"

He laughed again and suddenly he was holding her and she could smell him.   She could feel his heart beating against her cheek like that last time. Oh, she'd missed him.

"Home is here, Harmony," he said again. He kissed her hair, her cheek. "Home is you."

She met his mouth with hers and felt it, the passion and connection, and she couldn't stop her arms from wrapping around his neck as he held her tightly against him.

He pulled back and held her close. "I'm sorry I left. God, I shouldn't have left."

"I didn't… " She could barely get the words out. "I didn't give you a reason to stay."

He nodded and led her over to the bed. She needed to sit, that was for sure. Her dizziness was back and she doubted the baby was causing it.

"What about Boston, Rick?" she had to know. "What about Chapman?"

Rick shook his head. "'What about Bill' is what you mean, right?"

"All right." She licked her lips and tucked her hands under the thighs. "Yes. What about your father?"

"I told him to keep his job. It wasn't for me. Not anymore."

His eyes were crystal clear and bright. Of course, Ariel would want to check his aura. She could see the sincerity etched on his face, though. Oh, how she wanted to believe him.

"But it meant so much to you," she said. "For so long."

"I know. But I don't need it anymore." He took her

hands and held them. "I don't need corporate success or Bill's approval. I only need you."

She let his words sink in for a moment.

"Wow. That's a big change." She smiled at him. "Like the rec café."

His brows shot up. "You saw it?"

"Finally." Her cheeks heated with embarrassment. "It's beautiful, Rick. The colors. The style." She took a breath. "Thank you."

"For what?"

She tilted her head to one side. "You took care of my parents like I never could. I've never seen them so happy."

He nodded. "I've been checking in."

"Really? My mother didn't tell me."

He smiled. "They're a trip but the place is in good hands."

"I can see you've changed." She ran her fingers through the mussed hair at his temples. "But it's more than that. I can feel it. You're more relaxed, and... "

"And what?"

"You came back."

"Ah, sweetheart." He held her again. "My heart never

left."

She pulled back this time. "Your heart?"

"I love you, Harmony."

That did it. She turned and pinned him to her bed, right on top of her old quilt. His sweater was gone, his jeans thrown somewhere on the floor, and she had her way with him. His hands, his mouth, were everything she remembered. There was more. There was a tenderness she'd only felt for a few fleeting moments when they were together before. Now he held her, cherished her, and she was crazy to have him inside her.

"Rick, please."

He kissed her neck, her throat. Freeing her breasts from her bra was a two-second job and his mouth was on her. The sensation nearly made her climaxed.

He stilled and lifted his head. "Am I hurting you?"

She managed to open her eyes to find him staring up at her. "No." She swallowed and touched his face. "No."

When he left her for a moment—she could hear him rustling through his jeans' pocket—she stopped breathing. But then he was there, deep inside of her and she let go. Pleasure took her and she could hear his shout of release as if from far away.

Then he held her again, his arms wrapped around her and the soft quilt drifting over her. She breathed in. The scent of Rick and of their passion. Their love. Heaven.

"I love you, Harmony."

She caught her breath at last and looked into his eyes. His beautiful silver-gray eyes. "I love you."

He shifted and she cuddled closer to him. He deserved to hear it all. He'd given her his heart today, right?

"You're not the only one who's changed," she said.

"Hmm?" He kissed her hair and stroked her back. "Who else, then?"

"Me." She propped herself up on one arm and faced him. "I've changed. I'm ready to trust again. In you."

He grinned. "In us."

She had to tell him. Now. She took in a deep breath. "I'm pregnant."

He blinked. "You're pregnant? That's... Oh, God." *Please be happy. Please be happy.*

"Surprised?" she asked.

"Yeah." He grinned again. "But it's a good one." He

got up and knelt before her on the bed, tugging her to a sitting position. "Marry me, Harmony."

She must have heard him wrong. "What?"

"Marry me. Not just because of the baby. I love you and want to start our life right here in Cypress Corners."

"Do you… ?" She swallowed. "Do you mean it?"

"God, yes. I promise you this. Our child will never feel like I did."

Tears pricked her eyes. "Oh, Rick."

"Our child will always know he or she has my love and my full attention."

"You're going to be a wonderful father."

"Then marry me? Please?"

She knocked him over onto the bed again.

"Yes!"

Epilogue

Rick stepped out onto the porch and breathed in. It was October, but true autumn was months away. It was still warm, but in his cotton shirt and khaki shorts he was comfortable. He settled on the swing suspended from the porch ceiling and looked out over the park toward the lake, letting the breeze cool him as he sipped his coffee. He had about an hour before he had to show up at the Welcome Center. He was in charge of the Sales Office, and loved showing prospective residents and investors the benefits of living in a place like this.

Four years had passed since he first came to Cypress Corners, and the development still puzzled him. Pristine natural beauty and all the modern comforts blended together into a perfect place to make his life. His real life, not the one he'd left behind in Boston.

"Good morning!"

He turned to find Harmony walking up the sidewalk toward him. Wearing shorts and a tank top, her hair in a fat curly ponytail, she still made his mouth go dry. Talk about pristine natural beauty. Damn.

"Morning," he said. He put the coffee cup down on a side table and held out his arms. She came willingly, her and the little guy bounding along beside her. Their three-year-old son Nick.

Harmony sat beside him and held Nick on her lap. The boy was a looker, with black curls and hazel eyes. More than that, the kid knew Rick loved him.

"Daddy!"

Rick shifted and held his son close. He kissed the top of his head, feeling his soft curls with his cheek. "Hey, big guy. You and Mommy have a nice walk?"

Nick nodded. "We saw a lizard and Mommy said it was supposed to be eating that bug, so we didn't touch it. Over in the park there were three cranes as big as me!"

"Really? Cool."

"Miss Hettie gave me a seed pod." He held his hand out to show a slightly-crushed husk. "Mommy says we'll plant the seeds up near the café."

Harmony smiled. "Grandpa Max will enjoy those beans next summer."

Nick nodded and gave Harmony the seed husk. "I'm gonna play with my trucks."

And just like that he switched from nature boy to rough-and-ready little man as he hopped down. He hurried over to one corner of the wraparound porch and started to play with the oversized toy trucks and SUV's parked there. Rick watched him for a minute, shaking his head. Expensive gifts from Bill. The man would never learn.

He put his arm over Harmony's shoulders and they leaned back together on the swing. "I heard from Jake."

Harmony clicked her tongue. "I don't know why he's still at Chapman."

He shrugged. "He's still in grad school, too. Maybe he just can't figure out what he wants."

"It's a shame what your father did to all of you."

He just waved a hand. He wouldn't waste any time talking about Bill. His father was firmly in his past until he could come to terms with Rick's choices. With Rick's life.

"Jake's coming down next week," he went on. "Something about an extreme training camp."

She nodded. "I heard something about that at the Welcome Center. He's going to plan the project. Maybe that will give him some focus."

He was quiet for a moment. "Maybe he'll finally find

what I have."

She turned and smiled up at him. "And what's that, Rick Chapman?"

He grinned. "You know damn well, Harmony. I found you."

They shared a sweet kiss and she settled against his side once more. He thought about what he'd really found at Cypress Corners. Yes, he'd found the love of his life. The mother of his son. But he'd found an understanding, too. Life was full of contradictions, of choices. You had to know what was important and what wasn't. His life was like that. It was a life that needed balance.

He'd found his with Harmony.

About the Author

JoMarie DeGioia has been making up stories for as long as she can remember, and has spent years giving voice to the characters in her head. She's known Mickey Mouse from the "inside," has been a copyeditor for her town's newspaper, and a bookseller. She writes Historical and Contemporary Romances, along with Young and New Adult Fantasy stories. She divides her time between Central Florida and New England.

Discover other books

by JoMarie DeGioia

The Dashing Nobles series, including

More Than Passion

Pride and Fire

Just Perfect

More Than Charming

Connect with me online

Twitter: https://twitter.com/JoMarieDeGioia

Facebook:

https://www.facebook.com/JoMarie.DeGioia.Author

Website: www.jomariedegioia.com